I'm 16, I'm a witch, and I *still* have to go to school?

When I had a big history paper due, Salem suggested that I make the assignment come to life—literally— by traveling back in time to colonial times. But now Salem and I have been accused of using witchcraft— and we're guilty as charged! If we don't escape soon, the two of us will be history. . . .

My name's Sabrina and I'm sixteen. I always knew I was different, but I thought it was just because I lived with my strange aunts Zelda and Hilda while my divorced parents bounced around the world. Dad's in the foreign service. The *very* foreign service. He's a witch—and so am I.

I can't run to Mom—but *not* because she's currently on an archaeological dig in Peru. She's a mortal. If I set eyes on her in the next two years, she'll turn into a ball of wax. So for now I'm stuck with my aunts. They're hanging around to show me everything I need to know about this witch business. They say all I have to do is concentrate and point. And I thought fitting in was tough!

You probably think I have superpowers. Think again! I can't turn back time, and I'm on my own when it comes to love. Of course, there are some pretty neat things I *can* do—but that's where the trouble *always* begins. . . .

Sabrina, the Teenage Witch™ books

Available from ARCHWAY Paperbacks

Sabrina The Teenage Witch™

Salem on Trial

David Cody Weiss & Bobbi JG Weiss

AN ARCHWAY PAPERBACK
Published by POCKET BOOKS
New York London Toronto Sydney Tokyo Singapore

This book is a work of fiction. Names, characters, places and incidents are products of the author's imagination or are used fictitiously. Any resemblance to actual events or locales or persons living or dead is entirely coincidental.

AN ARCHWAY PAPERBACK *Original*

An Archway Paperback published by
POCKET BOOKS, a division of Simon & Schuster Inc.
1230 Avenue of the Americas, New York, NY 10020

ISBN: 0-671-01757-8

First Archway Paperback printing March 1998

10 9 8 7 6 5 4

AN ARCHWAY PAPERBACK and colophon are
registered trademarks of Simon & Schuster Inc.

SABRINA THE TEENAGE WITCH and all related titles, logos
and characters are trademarks of Archie Comics Publications, Inc.

Printed in the U.S.A.

IL: 5+

This one's for Lee, the man who put my money where his Mouse was.

—DCW

Salem on Trial

Chapter 1

Mrs. Hecht was a great believer in theories, which is why Sabrina Spellman sat directly in front of her teacher in history class. One of Mrs. Hecht's pet theories was that traditional methods of teaching had blind spots that needed correcting in order to keep subjects fresh and exciting for students. So while her students were seated in alphabetical order, it was a reverse alphabetical order, running from right to left as she faced the class. Her intent in this reorganization scheme was to pull the students whose last names normally put them in the back of every other classroom up to the front, where they could bask in the light of learning.

Sabrina believed in a couple of theories, too. The first was that she and Harvey Kinkle should be together as often as possible, and the second was that Libby Chessler spent most of her free time cooking up schemes to make Sabrina's life miserable. As Mrs. Hecht wrote in chalk on the blackboard "Westbridge: Colonial Period," Sabrina felt a new theory evolve in her head: Mrs. Hecht's theories were all part of a scheme by Libby to keep Harvey and Sabrina apart!

Thanks to Mrs. Hecht, Harvey—as a *K* for Kinkle—wound up sitting four seats directly behind Sabrina, and Libby—as a *C* for Chessler—sat right next to him. The front part of the alphabet outnumbered the back part in history class.

Even knowing that her close friend Jenny Kelly—as a fellow *K*—sat right behind Harvey and could keep watch on Libby for Sabrina, didn't make things better. More often than not it meant that Sabrina had to squirm through Jenny's reports of how Libby continually batted her eyes, smiled, and dropped every imaginable writing instrument on the floor to get Harvey's attention. Thankfully Harvey was unaware of this blatant flirting—cheerful naïveté being a yummier part of his charm—but Sabrina worried about his ability to resist Libby's social steamroller techniques. As it stood, Harvey and Libby sat side by side somewhere behind Sabrina where she couldn't stare dreamily at the one and keep an eagle eye on the other.

Frustration, major big-time.

"Knowing your environment is a grounding for knowing yourself," Mrs. Hecht pronounced as she continued writing on the blackboard, her oiled cornrows bobbing with each sweep of her chalk arm. "Since Westbridge is your home, its history helps shape who you are and how the world will perceive you when you leave here."

Sabrina looked out the second-floor windows at the panorama of Westbridge tumbling away from the hill on which the school sat. Unlike most of her classmates, Sabrina hadn't grown up there. She had spent most of her life moving around while her parents were together, and since they'd divorced a few years back, things had gotten even more hectic. Her mom was a mortal who, as an archaeologist, was forever hopping about the globe digging up other people's history. Her father was a witch and was currently living in a magic book that Sabrina kept on a stand by her bedside. Sabrina had come to the quiet New England town of Westbridge so she could have a stable home while finishing school.

As if discovering that she and her father's whole side of her family were witches, complete with supernatural powers, contributed to a stable environment!

Sabrina's aunts, Zelda and Hilda Spellman, were supposed to help train Sabrina in the use of her powers. Mortals were never supposed to find out how different the Spellman family really was. *A textbook example of stable teenage life,* thought Sabrina wryly. *Never let your friends know your true self. Still and all, Westbridge is a better place than many to grow up, I guess.*

"Surprisingly, less is known about the late colonial period in Westbridge than any other time in its history," Mrs. Hecht droned on, punctuating her sentences with sharp raps of chalk. "We know of its founding by Hezekiah Collins in 1676 and the early days of the township. The village grew in importance as a transport route after the western swamps were drained and cleared for crops. But around 1728, all mention of West Bridge, as it was known then, ceases for a few years." Dates and names marched along the blackboard, interrupted by a big question mark.

Sabrina continued gazing out the window. Cutting across the town at almost right angles to the river, a state road ran from Boston and the other coastal cities through Westbridge across an iron bridge.

The placid scene and the quiet murmur of Mrs. Hecht's voice lent a dreamlike air to the classroom, and Sabrina's eyes relaxed their focus. For a moment Harvey's face floated over the town view. *Wait a minute! That* is *Harvey!* Sabrina realized. If she leaned to her right, she could almost see Harvey reflected in the window glass—and he was smiling at Libby!

Sabrina tried for subtlety—twisting her head around as if she were merely stretching a stiff neck—but she was right in Mrs. Hecht's line of sight during the one moment the teacher turned back toward the class. "Miss Spellman," Mrs. Hecht said firmly, "am I boring you?"

Sabrina swiveled her head forward again and shot the teacher an innocent smile.

Mrs. Hecht returned to the blackboard and resumed her lecture. "We know that during the Revolution, West Bridge played a minor role in moving supplies and inflammatory pamphlets to patriot soldiers throughout the commonwealth right under the noses of the British troops. Paul Revere sent an engraved mirror to a local paper-maker as a thank-you gift for supplying free printing and paper."

Sabrina's eyes lit up. *That's it!* She reached into her backpack and slid out her compact. Flipping it open with one hand, she angled the mirror so she could see her own reflection. Concentrating, she pointed with her right index finger at the glass, smiling slightly as a spark leaped from her enameled nail. The mirror shimmered for an instant and then showed a crisp image of Harvey and Libby behind her as if no bodies sat in its way.

Harvey was staring at the blackboard with his usual glazed expression. He might have been asleep with his eyes open, but he *looked* as if he was concentrating. It was a skill Sabrina envied but couldn't practice this close to Mrs. Hecht. Libby, however, was folding up a note and reaching over to slip it under Harvey's ring binder.

Outraged, Sabrina jabbed her left hand over her right shoulder. In the magical reflection, a golden spark leaped from her index finger in an arc that landed on the note in Libby's hand. Keeping a wary eye on Mrs. Hecht's back, Libby didn't notice the spark as she tucked the note under Harvey's binder. But when she snatched her hand back, the note stuck to her fingers and rustled in the air. Surprised and annoyed, Libby shook her hand, making a louder snap of paper in the quiet classroom.

Sabrina smirked as she watched Libby struggle with the note that wouldn't let go. The cheerleader pulled frantically on the folded paper.

Mrs. Hecht whirled to face the class, zeroing in on the offending sound. Years of disciplinary reflexes kicked in, and she was looming over Libby before the cheerleader realized it. Sabrina pointed at the note again, canceling her first spell; it wouldn't do to have the teacher discover that the note was stuck firmly to Libby's hand.

Libby was doubly shocked. The teacher was suddenly in her face, plucking the note from her fingers, and the note, previously stuck to her hand, *actually let go!*

Mrs. Hecht unfolded the note. The crinkle of paper echoed in the absolute silence of the classroom. Another of Mrs. Hecht's pet theories was that private messages should be made public. Twenty-nine mouths gaped in anticipation as she read the note aloud.

" 'Harvey, this stuff is so dull. I'll never figure it out alone. Meet me after school to help me study?' " Mrs. Hecht's brown eyes bored twin holes into Libby. "Care to explain what is so dull about our town's history, Miss Chessler?"

Libby flushed for an instant before regaining her composure. *"I* don't find the subject boring at all, Mrs. Hecht," she said, her voice dripping sincerity. "I was passing that note for Sabrina."

Sabrina's outrage was almost ultrasonic. *"What?"*

Libby projected sadness and sympathy. "I told you it was wrong, but you insisted."

Mrs. Hecht had been teaching a long time. She arched one eyebrow at the brunette cheerleader and said dryly, "Very generous of you, Miss Chessler." She crumpled the note in her hand and strode back to the front of the room.

Behind Mrs. Hecht's back, Libby smirked at Sabrina, who knew it was a losing cause to pick a fight while the teacher was already peeved at her. She would have to accept whatever punishment the history teacher was going to assign her and figure out a way to get back at Libby later. *The story of my life in high school, it seems,* she grumbled to herself.

Throughout all this, Harvey had sat in silent confusion, which had not escaped Mrs. Hecht's attention. She faced the students, her face stern and calculating. Everyone fidgeted nervously. Finally she said, "This affair seems to be between you two young ladies, so I don't hold Mr. Kinkle and the rest of the class at fault."

The air hissed with sighs of relief.

Sabrina's compact still had the enchantment on it to show her Harvey and Libby. She saw the cheerleader's smug face cloud over as Libby realized that the finger of blame was still pointing at her. Mrs. Hecht continued, "I think it only appropriate, therefore, that both Miss Spellman and Miss Chessler make up for wasting class time by each writing a ten-page report on colonial Westbridge and presenting them on Monday."

Libby's reflection stared daggers at the back of Sabrina's head.

The bell rang and the students surged up from their seats like racehorses from the starting gate. Mrs. Hecht's raised hand froze them in place. Nobody left her class until she said so, and she was obviously not finished pronouncing doom.

"The reports will be based *fully* on written references—footnoted and with a complete bibliography, of course," she concluded. "Dismissed."

There goes my *weekend—and it's all* her *fault,* thought two angry girls in unison.

Chapter 2

☆

The Slicery was its usual Friday afternoon chaos of restless teenage bodies letting off steam from the school week and bubbling with weekend plans. That is, happy chaos reigned everywhere except at table 13, which had an invisible cloud of blue funk hovering over it. At table 13, Sabrina held forth on the perversity of the universe—at least the portion of it occupied by Libby Chessler.

"She actually thought she could get away with blaming *me* for that note," she fumed to Harvey and Jenny over pizza and a pitcher of cola.

"I don't understand," said Harvey, his eyebrows creasing a vertical line above his nose. "You *didn't* want me to come over and help you study?"

Sabrina was struck speechless. Jenny filled the silence. "Earth to Harvey. Libby wrote that note."

Harvey's pizza slice stopped midway between his

plate and his mouth. "Libby wanted me to help Sabrina study?" he asked in confusion. He took a bite and chewed both the pizza and the concept. "That doesn't sound like her," he said with his mouth still full.

Ever ready to commit herself to lost causes, Jenny tried to clue Harvey in on the subtleties of female in-fighting. "Harvey, Libby wanted you to come over and study with *her.*"

The rest of Harvey's pizza slice disappeared before he answered. "Then why did she say that Sabrina wrote the note? Wouldn't that have given me the wrong idea? I'd have wound up going to the wrong house." His puzzlement demanded almost a full glass of soda to lubricate his overheated brain. "Now I'm all confused. I need another slice of pizza." He slid off his stool and ambled toward the order window.

Sabrina watched as he walked away with unconscious grace and masculine simplicity. "Why do I want to hug him and strangle him at the same time?"

"That's what makes him Harvey," soothed Jenny. "And because you like him, Libby wants to take him away from you. Or at least spoil it for you." Jenny studied the world of social interaction the way physicists studied atomic structure, or astronomers the collisions of massive galaxies. "Look, the Libbys of the world get scared every time they see someone else being happy. It makes them jealous, and they feel that they're missing out on something. They can't stand the thought that someone else has something they don't. I, on the other hand, like seeing other people happy, because it cheers me up to know that even if I'm miserable, there is still happiness in the world."

Sabrina glanced sideways at her friend. "I'd ask you to explain all that again, but I don't think I'd understand it even then." Her head sank to the table, her blond hair narrowly missing a puddle of tomato sauce. "Anyway, I've got to figure out how I'm going to write a ten-page paper without any references."

"Why? I'm sure the school library has all the books you'll need."

"Mrs. Hecht was right about there not being much known about colonial Westbridge. The encyclopedias don't even mention it, and the only book about it was already checked out."

"What about the town library?"

"I asked Mrs. Nordling to check, but the reference copies were missing. Probably misfiled, she said."

Jenny was nothing if not doggedly resourceful. "Isn't her husband a writer who knows a lot of stuff?"

"About everything except Westbridge, it seems," Sabrina said with a wry face. "Mr. Nordling was there, and while his wife was checking for the books, he bent my ear for a half hour with a detailed lecture on storytelling."

Sabrina moodily placed two napkins on the table so she could keep her elbows clean while propping her chin on her hands. "I wonder if Mrs. Hecht would accept a hundred-page paper on the influence of cartoons instead of Westbridge's history?"

Jenny's gaze zeroed in on something over Sabrina's shoulder. "Don't look now, but I think I found the missing books."

Sabrina spun around on her stool. A brunette in a green-and-white cheerleader outfit strolled dramatically through the double doors of the Slicery carrying two library books under one arm.

"Libby!" Sabrina hissed. "That dirty little . . ."

Annoyed, she pointed at a tumbler on the table just to Libby's left. The glass tipped over, creating a small river of water and ice chips that splattered to the floor and slid under Libby's outstretched foot. The cheerleader suddenly found herself performing an unexpected and unrehearsed split.

The books tumbled as Libby broke her fall, but before Sabrina could magically whisk them closer, a male hand scooped them up. The lanky owner of the hand smoothly threw his other arm around Libby and pulled her back upright.

"Whoa!" exclaimed Jenny at the mini-drama. "Disaster Averted by Senior Save! Film at eleven."

Sabrina glared at her enemy's rescuer. "Who's Libby's 911?"

"His name is Henry Jones. The Third, no less."

Sabrina's stomach churned. "Not Encyclopedia Jones, the genius of Westbridge? The one who's already been accepted to Yale?"

"Bingo."

Sabrina's attempt to foil Libby and snatch up the necessary library books had backfired. The tall senior had already noticed the books' titles and opened them in delight. He flipped from page to page, offering rapid-fire comments on the texts. Libby recognized a potential asset and shifted into charm mode.

The cheerleader didn't have witch powers, but nothing Sabrina knew how to do could have bewitched the senior any more quickly or neatly. "How can she smile that wide without her face cracking?" she asked Jenny in mock revulsion.

Jenny was more interested in the poor fish caught on Libby's hook. "He looks as if he's adding drool to the tomato-sauce stains on his shirt."

"I'm sunk. Libby not only clipped the only reference works *in* town *on* the town, but she's about to get the smartest kid in school to write the paper for her!"

Jones took the books from the cheerleader with a smile that belied his reputed intellectual prowess. Tucking them under one bony arm, he scurried around the table to escort Libby to the door.

Sabrina glowered at the exiting couple. "She's leaving with him *and* the books," she complained, her voice rising in despair. "Why aren't there Library Police you can call for times like these?"

Harvey sauntered back to the table with four slices of pizza piled on a paper plate. "You guys look bummed. Your pizza get cold?" He offered his plate. "You can share mine."

"No, thanks. I'm going to fail Mrs. Hecht's class because someone stole all of Westbridge's history," Sabrina moaned.

Harvey looked shocked. "That's not true. There's history all around you. This place, for example." He waved at the solid brick walls of the Slicery and its massive oak beams. "It started out as the town's original tavern and meeting hall. The video room used to be a jail cell. And there are root cellars and storage tunnels under here that were later used to smuggle escaped slaves to Canada during the Civil War. Think of it—a pizza place that used to be a station on the Underground Railroad."

Jenny was impressed at this sudden show of knowledge. "Do you sleep on a history book instead of a pillow?"

"Naw, my dad had the contract to fumigate this place last year. He and I crawled all over and under the Slicery setting traps and spraying." Harvey shook his head as he took a huge bite of pepperoni and cheese. "You wouldn't believe how many bugs there were under the kitchen," he said around the mouthful.

Sabrina nervously eyed the Slicery, the comfortable hangout suddenly transformed into an ancient den of treachery, imprisonment, and things scuttling under the floorboards. She slid from her stool. "I've gotta go," she said, backing toward the door. "Somehow I don't have an appetite anymore."

☆

Chapter 3

☆

The houses along Collins Road were genteel survivors from an earlier age. Decked out in gingerbread and scrollwork, the old Victorians were massive by modern standards and sat on generous lots shaded by sturdy old trees. Sabrina scuffled her way up the walk to the Spellman house, oblivious to the riot of colors in branches above her.

She pushed the oversize front door open and trudged toward the broad staircase that led to the second floor. She wanted nothing more than to slink into her bedroom and mope the weekend away. As she lifted a foot to climb the stairs, a dark blur sped under it, breaking her stride and making her grab the banister to keep from toppling over.

"Salem!" Sabrina yelled at the black cat who froze midway up the steps. "Are you crazy? You could have tripped me!"

15

"It's your aunts who have gone crazy," Salem replied. He was actually a witch who had been sentenced to be a cat for a hundred years as punishment for a failed attempt to take over the world. Disrespect was one of his faults before he was transformed, and being a cat hadn't improved his attitude. "I can't bear to watch."

In spite of her glum mood Sabrina had to know more. "Excuse me?"

"They're out in the backyard burying perfectly good fish!" he hissed as if this were a capital offense. Then he zipped upstairs without explaining further.

Witchcraft was the norm in the Spellman household. Sabrina had come home to stranger things, like impromptu Mexican fiestas complete with a giant flan, temporary dates made out of no-bake man-dough, and a literary discussion group made up of Aunt Zelda and a couple of brains in big glass jars. Anything was possible.

Sabrina changed her mind about hiding in her room and instead walked briskly through the brick-walled kitchen and the glassed-in porch toward the backyard.

Lush and neatly landscaped, the Spellman backyard was dominated by a gnarled and towering oak tree. Its trunk was easily six feet in diameter, but about fifteen feet up, it divided into four sections only slightly narrower than the base. The broad spread of the branches, with the open space in the middle, had earned the tree its nickname, the

Crown Oak, and as far as Sabrina knew it was hundreds of years old.

At that, it was younger than the two women under it, though neither of them looked their actual age.

Hilda, the younger sister, was dressed in a classic sixties pinup sun outfit—neon pink stretch Capris with a cotton top tied to display a tanned midriff, teardrop sunglasses with rhinestone accents, a floppy straw hat with a band that matched the lemon scarf around her neck, floral-pattern gloves and open-toed high-heel sandals that kept sinking into the freshly turned dirt beneath her feet.

Zelda, as befit her role as the older and more mature sister, wore practical jeans over sturdy shoes, a red checked flannel shirt, sturdy canvas gloves, and a paisley kerchief that held back her short pale hair.

An area running the width of the backyard and surrounding the Crown Oak had been marked off with stakes and string. A portion of it had already been dug up, and Zelda was enthusiastically piercing more grass with a pitchfork, pushing it deep with her foot and forking it over to expose rich, dark loam. Hilda followed behind, swatting at the overturned chunks of sod with a hoe in a rather haphazard effort to break up the clods. There was a bucket of fish parts nearby, but Sabrina's nose told her that if they were Salem's idea of "perfectly good fish" she'd never accept the cat's invitation to lunch.

Sabrina cleared her throat to get her aunts' attention. "Is this some special ritual that I haven't been told about?"

Hilda smiled at her perkily. "Yes. The specially initiated call it gardening."

"We're getting the flower bed ready," explained Zelda, pausing to wipe sweat from her brow. "The ground has to be prepared and fertilized; then we can plant the seeds deep before the rains come."

Hilda swatted another dirt clod with an overhand stroke. "It'll take us all weekend. Don't be afraid to lend a hand."

"How about I lend a finger instead?" Sabrina pointed at an undug section of garden. Like a carpet, the grass started rolling itself up, exposing dirt underneath.

In unison, Zelda and Hilda pointed their gloved fingers at the sod roll, canceling out Sabrina's magic and restoring the grass to its original state in an instant. "Some things are best done the old-fashioned way," Zelda said firmly.

Hilda nodded her head in agreement. "I don't usually believe in hard work, but with plants it makes a difference."

"You appreciate the natural magic of gardening when you get your hands dirty doing it. The gardener gets as much out of the process as the plants do. Besides, there's always the chance we'll find a bottle or plate from the old days buried here. We've found some valuable collectibles that way."

Hilda held out her hoe. "We have a pretty big

garden that has to be dug almost two feet down. You're welcome to help."

Sabrina was in no mood to deal with a rapid-fire aunt attack. "Thanks, but I have a ten-page paper to write this weekend."

"Your loss," said Hilda. "When the Crown Oak is surrounded by flowers, we'll bask in the miracle of renewal that's been happening throughout history."

"And *before*," added Zelda. "Nature's a force stronger than any witch magic."

"I'll still pass," said Sabrina, turning back to the house. A sudden light dawned in her head, and she whirled to face her aunts again. "Speaking of history, you guys were around in colonial Westbridge, weren't you?"

The two women conjured up tall, frosty lemonades. "Of course we were around, dear," said Zelda, taking a sip.

"We just weren't *here*," qualified Hilda. Her lemonade had a little parasol leaning over the rim of the glass.

Sabrina was confused. "You weren't?"

Zelda shot a teasing look at her sister. "Hilda was one of Johann Sebastian Bach's groupies about then. She followed him from concert to recital. As I recall, she was especially fond of his chamber works."

"I was studying composition," objected Hilda, stung. Then she smiled nastily and said to Sabrina, "You might like to know that your aunt Zelda was tossing apples at Sir Isaac Newton in England during all of that period."

Zelda's cheeks reddened. "I only made one apple drop. After all, someone had to put him on the right track. Anyway, if I hadn't been there to take notes, he never would have published anything!"

"So why didn't you write them in English to start with?"

"Anybody who was anybody published in Latin in those days."

"Not musicians. We used the most romantic language of all—Italian."

"Germans writing operas in Italian? Not *my* idea of romance."

"What would someone with her nose in a book all the time know about romance?"

Sabrina scuttled back to the house with a quick, "Uh, thanks for the help, guys," which she knew her aunts didn't even hear.

She found Salem in her bedroom staring fixedly at one wall. As far as she could tell, there was absolutely nothing to see there—no bug, no spot, no beam of light, not even a dust mote, but she was used to this kind of behavior from the cat. Sometimes she thought he did it just to see if he could get the humans to stare, too, so that he could have a good laugh at having suckered them in.

She was in no mood for games today, though. "Beat it, cat," she growled. "This room isn't big enough for both of us to sulk in. Unless, of course, you can write me a ten-page paper on the history of Westbridge."

"Sorry. World domination was my field of interest, not the study of suburban backwaters," Salem drawled. "Have you tried the library?"

Sabrina snatched up a pillow and threw it at him. Salem dodged the fluffy missile and fled to safety. "Aren't we a little touchy," he called from under the bed. "I take it something happened in today's episode of *Teen Angst?*"

Sabrina flopped backward onto the bed and poured out her tale of misery and betrayal. Salem slunk out of hiding and joined her on the comforter, lying on his back with all four paws pointed at the ceiling, occasionally allowing the teenager to soothe herself by rubbing his belly.

"So what's the problem?" he demanded, blinking in surprise. "You need to know about Westbridge in colonial times—go there."

☆

Chapter 4

☆

"Excuse me?" Sabrina said to the cat on her bed. "I know I'm a witch, but I thought we couldn't mess with time."

"Witches can't turn back time, except in special cases," Salem agreed, stroking his whiskers lightly with his left paw, "but there's nothing that says we can't *travel* through time. I've got four temporal-traveler bonus days in my account at the travel agency. You could use them to travel back to Westbridge in the year of your choice and get your history firsthand."

"There's an agency that books *time* trips?" Sabrina was still new to the unique behind-the-scenes resources available to witches.

"Of course. Did you think I planned on taking over the world without studying the would-be conquerors of the past?" Salem's eyes glazed over with inner visions of the vast panorama of history. "I went back to watch Alexander the Great, Julius Caesar, Attila the Hun, and Garbonzo Grosskopf in action."

"Garbonzo Grosskopf? Who's that?"

"You won't find him in your history books," Salem said, swatting at a dust mote drifting by. "That's why he's worth studying. You can learn as much from the losers as you can from the winners." He carefully examined his paw to see if he had caught anything, "The man was ahead of his time, I'll give you that. He established a monopoly on the world's oil supply and tried holding it hostage."

"Sounds like a plan to me."

Salem snorted. *"Olive* oil, not petroleum. This was in the sixth century. He was outmaneuvered by the butter cartels."

"Oh." With a thoughtful expression, Sabrina threw herself back onto the pile of pillows and stared up at the ceiling, trying to digest the new possibilities open to her. "So I can visit any time in the past I want, just like a sight-seeing tour?"

"Not exactly," Salem qualified.

Sabrina regarded the cat from half-lidded eyes. "Why am I not surprised there's a catch?"

"No catch," protested Salem, "just no tour. You go back by yourself and live just as they did for as long as you're there."

Sabrina tried to imagine herself in a world without TV, radio, CDs, and pizza parlors, a society established by people who wanted the freedom to live the way they thought proper—and persecuted anybody who disagreed with them. Sudden realization kicked in. "Wait a minute—they were *Puritans* back then! Those weren't exactly witch-friendly people. Remember when my history class went to that re-creation of Salem Village and I wound up on trial for witchcraft? Playacting was scary enough—no way I want it to happen for real."

"No sweat. The Witches' Council is real touchy about anybody changing history, so all witches who travel back have their powers sealed so they can't make trouble."

"No powers, no hassle." Sabrina pondered this. "It sounds good, but I just don't know. . . ."

"You don't dream of world conquest if you don't believe that your ideas are better than anybody else's." Salem was determined to make a sale here. "Look, I *guarantee* that nothing bad will happen. Have I ever lied to you?"

He realized he'd asked the wrong question when Sabrina pinned him with an accusing glare. "You told me that the USDA recommended cats have five servings of tuna per day."

Salem sniffed in dismissal. "That wasn't a lie. I just misunderstood what I heard on TV. Happens to people all the time." He cocked his head at Sabrina. "Check out your alternatives: either join your aunts and grub in the dirt or have your face rubbed in it on Monday by Libby."

With a sigh, Sabrina shuffled off the bed and

went to stare out her bay window. Down in the backyard, Zelda was in the process of dumping a glop of fish guts into a hole that Hilda had dug. That sight was all Sabrina needed. She spun around and marched to the linen closet door to find Salem already there, looking smug and superior.

Although it appeared to be an ordinary upstairs storage area, the linen closet in the Spellman house doubled as an entrance to the magical Other Realm. It also served as a shortcut, allowing witches to travel vast distances instantaneously. So far, Sabrina had been to the Witches' Council, which was ten million light-years away, and to Mars, which was, astronomically speaking, right around the corner. The closet also led to places that didn't seem to exist anywhere in the normal universe, like Limbo. All one did was close the door and walk forward.

Sabrina looked down at Salem in sudden confusion. "How do we get to this time-travel agency, anyway?"

"Over the linens and through the percales," he said, trotting inside.

A brilliant flash and a thunderous *swoosh* later, Sabrina and Salem stepped out onto a carpet of fluffy cumulus clouds. A featureless blue void stretched as far as the eye could see in all directions. The only two objects on the cloud-floor were the closet door behind them and an antique ticket window directly ahead.

Technically speaking, the window wasn't *on* the clouds; it floated at about eye level without visible support. Above it floated an equally gravitationally challenged wooden sign, bearing the words "Möbius Trips" in pink neon letters. As Sabrina stared at the sign, the words changed to "Whenever You Go, You'll Be There in Time." After a moment it changed back to its original wording.

"Somebody paid big for that slogan," remarked Salem acidly. "If they caught him."

The sliding glass panel in the window was shut, but there was a ticket dispenser with the instruction "Take a Number" printed on it. Sabrina pulled the protruding paper tab and tore off a ticket. It bore the symbol for infinity, a sideways stretched-out figure eight.

"Just a little temporal humor," boomed a hearty voice.

Sabrina blinked in surprise at the window, which snapped open to reveal a moon-faced man who hadn't been there an instant before. He wore an old-fashioned chalk-striped shirt with pulled-up sleeves held by black armbands. A green visor shaded his eyes. "When do you want to go?" he asked, resting his elbows on the window counter. The rest of his body simply wasn't there, hidden behind a solid counter that simply wasn't there either. It was very strange, but then, Sabrina was used to strange things these days.

Salem jumped up on the counter to take charge of the situation. "I don't want to go anywhen. I'm

Salem Saberhagen and I have four bonus days in my account. I want my friend to take a two-day trip back 250 years and have it charged to me."

"Sorry, can't do it," said the clerk. He stared past the cat and bellowed, "Next!"

Sabrina looked around, but there wasn't anybody else in sight.

"Can you tell me *why* it can't be done?" Salem was being as polite as possible, for a cat who by nature believed that the world existed solely to satisfy feline expectations.

"Yep," said the clerk agreeably.

Silence hung in the air for a moment. "Well?" said Salem finally.

"Well, what?" countered the clerk.

"Are you going to answer my question?"

"Did."

Salem snorted. "No, you didn't!"

The clerk wagged a finger infuriatingly in front of the cat's nose. "I answered every question you asked. What more do you want?"

"I want an explanation why Sabrina can't have a trip charged to my account."

"Sure thing," the clerk said, irritatingly cheerful. "Just as soon as you ask me."

Salem's tail became a black bottle-brush. One lip curled up, baring a sharp fang. "I *have* been asking," he hissed.

"Haven't," said the clerk, apparently amused to no end by the debate.

"Wait, I think I understand," Sabrina interrupted. She spoke carefully to the clerk. *"Why* can't Salem charge a trip for me to his account?"

The clerk's eyes twinkled merrily as he replied, "Not allowed."

Sabrina nodded her head. She now had an idea of how the clerk's mind worked. "What *exactly* isn't allowed?"

"Using an account to pay for someone else to travel."

"At all?"

The clerk positively beamed. "Yes and no."

Sabrina thought hard. "Under what conditions *would* it be allowed?"

The clerk snapped his fingers and a long, closely printed document appeared next to the window, hanging in midair. "Section IX, sub-heading 32, paragraph 104: 'Bearer of temporal-transit passage may use accrued applicable account credits to transport additional temporal-transit travelers for accompaniment purposes only.'"

"And in English that means . . . ?"

The clerk considered Salem for a moment. The cat was glaring murderously at him, flexing his claws into the counter. Several deep scratches already marred the varnished wood surface. The clerk grinned maliciously. "If he wants you to go, he has to go himself and take you as his guest."

"What?" yowled Salem. "Me go back to 1728? Canned food for *humans* wasn't invented until the 1800s, let alone Finicky Cat Lobster-Tuna Delite!"

"Maybe they'll let you bring some along," Sabrina offered, trying to keep the peace.

"Nope," interrupted the clerk. "Contraband. Can't take anything back that might change history."

Salem snorted, and Sabrina's shoulders slumped in defeat. "Guess we aren't going, then. Thanks for trying anyway, Salem." She scooped the cat off the counter into her arms.

"Wrong," boomed the clerk. When Sabrina stared in blank confusion at him, he added, "According to my records, you already went to Westbridge in 1728."

Sabrina almost dropped Salem. "What? When did I do that? How do you *know* that?"

A left-handed gesture by the clerk caused a computer screen and keyboard to materialize. A list of reservations and itineraries scrolled across the screen at blurring speed. Tapping the display, the clerk explained, "Got every time trip that will ever have happened recorded right here. This says you left exactly ten minutes from now, after I gave you your ticket. Returned the same day you left. That's one of the tricks of time travel. Sorry, you can't come back before you go."

With Salem in her arms, Sabrina felt like a twisted version of Dorothy transported to Oz. "Now I'm really confused. What if I changed my mind and decided not to go now?"

The clerk's expression turned ominous for the

first time. "You'd have to tell it to Drell. Y'see, since you've already made your trip into the past, what you're *going* to do is already history. If you don't go, you'll change history. Drell and the council will have hated that, and the one unchangeable thing in the universe is Drell's anger. Just ask your cat."

"You *would* bring that up," Salem snarled. Drell was the one who had turned him into a cat as punishment for trying to take over the world.

Sabrina had also crossed Drell a few times during her short witch career. She wasn't foolish enough to think he'd be any less fastidious about the rules than the clerk was about grammar and tense. "Well, I guess if I've already gone, I'll have to go ahead and go." Her eyes rolled with the intricacy of trying to talk about time travel. "Boy, does this stuff get confusing!"

"That's why I insist on people saying *exactly* what they mean." The Clerk nodded. He held out a hand, and a contract appeared in it. "Two days in 1728, two travelers, paid by accrued bonus days—total cost, four days. I'll need your paw-print here, please."

Salem touched his right forefoot to the paper at the indicated space. An impression of his paw appeared in red on the contract.

"And here and here and here," continued the clerk, flipping pages rapidly, "and *here.*"

Salem complied, and the contract vanished. The

clerk withdrew into the window. "Come on in and see what you're going to have worn."

Sabrina heard a door opening and suddenly found herself and Salem in a different-color void—pastel yellow this time—facing a silver-framed full-length mirror.

The ticket clerk popped into existence next to her, full-bodied this time, and consulted a large open book on a pedestal that had appeared with him. "Seventeen twenty-eight," he muttered while flipping pages. "Seventeen . . . ah! Here it is—1728. West Bridge, a settlement in the royal colonies of New England. You'll need a North American colonial Puritan style seven-B." He peeled off a decal of a woman's dress from one page of the book. Holding the picture firmly between finger and thumb he shook it three times and threw it at Sabrina. The picture of the dress hit her and was transformed into a perfectly fitted outfit.

Gone were her slim pants and fitted shirt. Looking at her reflection in the mirror, Sabrina saw that she was wearing a dark blue smocklike gown over a linen chemise with bloused sleeves. A stiff black corset hugged her torso. The gown reached to the tops of her shoes, which were very sturdy and had brass buckles on the outer sides. Her shoulder-length blond hair was swept up and pinned under a raw-linen mobcap, a sort of stylish bag with pleats flaring out from a waxed twine drawstring.

The clerk pursed his lips as he inspected

Sabrina's outfit. He held his hands together at the thumbs and made a pulling-apart motion. Sabrina's breath was squeezed violently out of her as the bodice tightened and narrowed her waist by four inches.

"Is . . . this," she gasped, "necessary?"

"Oh, yes," replied the clerk, pleased with the change. "At that, you're still a little wide for the period. Most girls start wearing stays at six or seven."

"Bet you'll never envy a supermodel again," snickered Salem, who had decided that the only comfortable place in this void for a cat to be was draped across the top of the mirror frame.

"One last detail and you're ready to go," said the clerk. He clapped his hands twice, and a giant candle, bigger than Sabrina, appeared over her head. The wick burst into brilliant purple flame, and the candle tilted, dripping hot wax down onto her. Instead of burning, however, the wax drops dissolved into a transparent glowing film that surrounded Sabrina for a brief instant before vanishing. "Sealing wax," explained the clerk. "To keep you from using your powers as long as you're out of your normal time period."

"It's the only thing that prevented me from becoming Salem Augustus, emperor of Rome," said Salem, baring his teeth at the melting drops.

Two more handclaps from the clerk and the candle vanished along with the mirror, much to Salem's surprise and dismay. A five-foot drop is no

big deal to a cat, but they usually like to prepare for
it first. He made a three-point landing—front paws
and nose—on the clouds.

The clerk beckoned with an extended finger, like
a New Yorker hailing a cab, and a black-and-red
lacquered coach door appeared in front of Sabrina.
It swung open to reveal the inside of a coach
containing facing leather seats and windows on the
far side that showed green woodlands moving by.
The interior rocked to a motion that existed somewhere—somewhen other than the yellow void.
"Your coach is approaching your stop, Mistress
Spellman. I suggest you board immediately."

Sabrina scrambled to pick up Salem and get into
the coach. She found it nearly impossible to bend
over in such a tight bodice, and it was worse trying
to sit down.

The door started to close by itself, but Sabrina
blocked it with her shoulder. "Wait!" she yelled to
the clerk. "Where's my luggage?"

"What luggage you'll have needed is in your
traveling bag. See you later!" He waved good-bye.
His gesture magically pushed Sabrina back into her
seat and slammed the coach door shut.

☆

Chapter 5

☆

Sabrina stared out of the rocking coach as it bounced and jounced its way along a rutted dirt road that cut through a forest, a kind of forest Sabrina had seen only in Robin Hood movies.

Unlike the New England of 1998, which was gradually turning into a solid expanse of strip malls and suburbs, this New England lay swathed in old-growth forest in its prime. Tall, with massive trunks and sprawling canopies, the birch, maple, oak, and walnut trees had lived undisturbed for centuries. There was a surprising amount of clear space between their lower branches and the ground, making the forest look like an enormous green hall supported by great bark pillars. Sunlight pierced the dense foliage above in isolated shafts or in the infrequent clearings created by the felling of one of those ancient giants by a storm or by mere gravity.

Sabrina would have marveled at the raw majesty of such a setting, but she was too busy getting rattled and tossed around the coach like dice in a cup. Wishing that their crude vehicle possessed front-wheel drive and dual suspension, to say nothing of a good four-speaker stereo system, Salem concentrated on just maintaining his balance, claw-clutching the leather seat for dear life. Whenever a particularly deep rut tipped the coach violently to the left or right, he ripped deep gouges before he got a fresh grip. "I'm beginning to remember why I hated being in the past!" he yowled.

"I'm g-going to b-be a mass of b-b-bruises by the time we g-g-get th-there," Sabrina managed to say. "We m-must be miles from civ-civiliza-za-*tion!*"

It came as a complete surprise when the coach bore left around a short curve in the road and entered a wide, clear-cut area that cupped twenty or more buildings between the woods and a river.

Most of the structures were constructed of heavy timbers much like a rough version of clapboard. Many were two-story houses with clusters of out-buildings flanking them, snug or ramshackle depending on the owners' wealth. Roofs were pitched at an extreme angle to survive heavy winter snows without collapsing. Most of the larger houses had end gables and dormers with casement windows to let in the buttery light. All but the poorest boasted brightly painted window frames and other trim work. In the center of town stood a handful of buildings constructed entirely of brick, though every house had at least one brick chimney.

In sharp contrast to the clear air in the forest, the town sat under a battalion of smoke columns, combining into a sooty pall that slowly drifted westward beyond the river. A brew of woodsmoke, manure, rotting vegetation, and animal smells assaulted Sabrina's nose as she leaned out of the window to get a better look. "Gackk!" she choked when she finally got her breath back.

"Welcome to the good old days everyone talks about," drawled Salem, who as a cat had a far more sensitive nose than Sabrina and was nearly cross-eyed at the olfactory overload. "Oh, those carefree days before air pollution. We had to travel downwind of horses, and I don't even want to talk about pigpens. I just hope we don't park downwind of a cow."

The distance from the edge of the woods to the center of town was short. Sabrina barely had time to catch a first impression of the place before the coach rattled to a halt in front of an imposing brick building that had a signpost bearing the painted image of a man sawing wood. The coach rocked as the driver stepped down from his box.

"This here be ther common 'ouse of West Bridge, mistress," said a voice that was familiar in spite of the coarse English accent. Under a dusty black tricorn hat, the clerk's face smiled at Sabrina and Salem. Giving them a wink, he opened the door, extending a hand to help the young witch clamber down from the tall coach.

"We would have had an easier ride if you'd levitated the—*mmmf!*" Salem's complaint was silenced as the clerk snatched the cat by the scruff of his neck and thrust him into a wicker basket.

"Best kype yer cat tooked away heer. There's thos'ud tyke exception ter his color, heerabouts," the clerk/driver said loudly. Hissing through his teeth he added, "And some besides me that would like to strangle him. I should have sealed his mouth along with your powers."

He thrust the basket into Sabrina's arms and hoisted himself back up to the driver's box. Rummaging under a canvas tarp covering the roof of the coach, he pulled out a bulky leather satchel, which he threw down at Sabrina's feet. "We begs yer pardon agin, mistress, fer separatin' yer and yer loogage. But me broother'll be by in a day or twa, ter help yer finish yer journey fra New York ter Boston."

In the hectic excitement of booking her travel through time, Sabrina had never given a thought to the necessity for a cover story. The clerk had just given her a reminder of that and established a plausible reason for her temporary presence in West Bridge for anyone within earshot.

Once reminded, Sabrina wanted to catch a minute or two with the clerk to confirm further details, but the man was already cracking his whip and starting up the horses. Without looking back, he drove the carriage in a wide circle and headed back to the forest. In moments he was gone, leaving Sabrina alone in an alien society with no money, no supplies, and a wicker basket full of ticked-off cat.

She looked up and down the main street, if that was indeed the correct term for the rutted stretch of dirt separating an uneven line of houses and shops. Most of the buildings fronted directly on the street without benefit of front yards. The few that didn't had gardens planted on either side of the path up to the front door. The town didn't seem to have any real system of streets and alleys, just paths worn through the grass growing around boundary fences. Sometimes the grass was trimmed in the empty spaces, and Sabrina could see the mowers—several shaggy sheep ambling from house to house.

The sheep were not the only livestock running loose. It seemed that every yard had its flock of chickens pecking away in the grass. A half-dozen piglets ran squealing along a path, herded by children with a dog yapping at the corkscrew piggy tails.

She picked up her luggage, grunting at the weight of the heavy leather bag, and headed for the open door of the tavern.

"Well," Sabrina muttered softly to the cat in the basket, "I guess I can deal with this. What can go wrong in two days?"

Chapter 6

☆

It was darker than she'd expected inside the brick building, and her eyes took a moment to adjust. What light there was shone through relatively small windows composed of diamond-shaped panes of glass set in a lattice frame. The glass had a curious pattern of concentric circles around a central dimple that further cut down on the light passing through.

The room was eerily familiar. *Why, it's practically the Slicery, only a little different,* she realized. The front door stood in the same place, but the great fireplace opposite it was pretty much where the brick pizza ovens would be in 250 years. True, the long wainscoted counter ran the length of one wall instead of running in front of the ovens, but the small room that would become the video game room lay in its future location, only blocked by a barred door in this time.

A man and woman talking at the counter were the only other people in the whole place. Sabrina studied them, trying to figure out who she needed to talk to in order to book a room in the tavern.

The man, a human beanpole with a beaky nose and rather large ears, was clothed all in black—a faded, worn black—with the exception of a white linen shirt and stockings, yellowed a bit from age. His black leather shoes sported big iron buckles, his breeches and waistcoat were made of well-worn wool, and his frock coat, with its large turnback cuffs and lapels lined with buttons and buttonholes, revealed shiny spots at the elbows. On his head perched a rather cheap-looking wig tied in a black bow at the back. Snowy speckles of the flour used to whiten his wig flecked the shoulders of his coat and gathered in small piles on his neckcloth like dandruff.

He was trying to loom with dignity over the small woman behind the bar, but Sabrina thought he just looked swaybacked. He said loudly, "Goody Watkins! You know that it is my sworn duty as magistrate of this town to ensure, by personal examination, the quality of the goods you provide to your guests."

Goody Watkins stared back at the magistrate with natural dignity bolstered by a double heaping of scorn. "It seems more than passing strange, Magister Blackpoole, that you feel the call of duty strongest as I prepare meals and the examination be free. I see you but rarely when meals are served and there is money to be paid."

She stood a little taller than Sabrina despite being of middle age. A white linen apron partly covered her indigo dress, and her dark hair had been tied up under an embroidered kerchief topped with a flat green hat that matched her bodice.

The argument seemed to Sabrina to be an ongoing one, because Goody Watkins protested no further but produced a bowl of some kind of stew from under the counter and handed it to Magister Blackpoole, who, supplying his own horn spoon, took it to a nearby table and began wolfing it down.

The hostess spied Sabrina at the door and cried out in a loud, cheery voice, "Ho! A stranger comes! Be welcome in the Woodcutter Tavern and in our fair town. How may I be of service to you?"

Before Sabrina could answer, there was a commotion behind her and she was nearly bowled over by a breathless young woman who came barreling into the tavern. This girl, who elbowed Sabrina aside, was followed by another young woman. Both were about the same age as Sabrina, but their clothing spoke of a vast difference in status.

The impatient girl was decked out in the finest clothing Sabrina had seen yet, with cascades of delicate lacework over heavily embroidered materials making up the common assembly of gown, bodice, and apron. Despite the workerlike badge of apron, it was clear to everyone that this girl did as little work as possible, except perhaps on her attire and appearance. Dark-eyed and self-assured, she acted as if she owned the room and it was only by courtesy that she noticed the lesser beings in it.

The other girl was plainly a hard worker from a lower class. Her dress was neat and clean but patched in places, her apron worn and frayed. Work-callused hands with strong, narrow fingers impatiently waved several square pieces of paper in an attempt to get the finer girl to notice them. The only things not subdued about her were her hair and eyes. The former was a torrent of flaming curls, barely contained in a green lacework hairnet, while the latter displayed as much fire and unruliness as her hair. "Mistress Chestler," she pleaded, "will you please stop a moment and tell me *why* the wallpaper dissatisfies you?"

The hostess and the magistrate both nodded their greetings to Mistress Chestler, but she ignored them to whirl upon the other girl and reply snappishly, "It is the pattern, Mistress Kelleigh! It simply will not do!" She pulled the paper samples roughly out of the redhead's hands. "This design is obviously a *baronial crown!* I most particularly ordered a crown pattern in the *imperial* style!"

Sabrina could see that the papers had a repeated pattern of pale maroon crowns on a buff background, but she didn't know enough about heraldry to distinguish ranks. The line work was quite fine and nicely printed, though.

Mistress Kelleigh did not let her lower station prevent her from arguing with her social better. "I printed from the blocks that you had 'Prentice Harvard carve. He had but the reference you provided him. Your quarrel cannot be with me. I have provided you with the work you contracted."

"But that is not the pattern I wish to have on my chamber walls! I will have imperial crowns and no less!"

"Then you are forswearing our bargain?"

Before Mistress Chestler could answer yes, Magister Blackpoole looked up from his now empty bowl. "A bargain is a contract, Mistress Libbeth Chestler. A failure to honor a contract is punishable under law. It is a dishonor to the work, and work is our supreme effort. Our town is founded upon work, excepting only the Sabbath, when, since work is forbidden then, we must work at not working. If you break contract with Mistress Juniper Kelleigh, I must fine you and collect upon the spot."

"Of which you will certainly keep half," sneered Libbeth.

"Of course," agreed Magister Blackpoole without shame. "It is the prerogative of my position as magistrate."

Libbeth chewed this over for a moment, obviously not willing to allow herself to be shamed and fined. She set her mind and turned to snap fiercely at Juniper, "I will accept these—pending correction of the blocks and the delivery of the balance of the sheets with the correct *imperial* crowns." She handed the sheets back. "I could not refuse the fine work of my dearest Harvard."

"Hmph" was all that Juniper had to say in reply. She dropped the bundle of paper on the counter and left the tavern.

With that bit of business taken care of, Libbeth wasted no time in getting back to her original topic. "I saw a coach pass through," she addressed the hostess and the magistrate. "Has my maidservant arrived?"

"A stranger has come to town, but who she is and what her business might be is hers to explain," stated Goody Watkins.

Everyone turned to stare at Sabrina. "Hi," she said uncomfortably. "I'm Sabrina—er, Mistress Spellman. I'm just sorta . . . passing through."

"On what business?" asked Goody Watkins sharply. "No honest woman travels abroad without company, without making arrangements along the way. And we have no place for any other kind."

"Well, actually I'm here by accident. I was traveling from New York to Boston to see my, uh, father. And there was this mix-up, you see, and I got on the wrong coach and wound up here. Everything will be straightened out in a couple of days."

"You are from New York, you say?" said Goody Watkins, as if the very name left a bad taste in her mouth.

Magister Blackpoole shared some suspicions about Sabrina's alleged city of origin. "They allow the Dutch down there still, do they not?" he demanded, peering down his beaky nose at her.

Sabrina remembered that New York had once been Nieuw Amsterdam, a Dutch colony, before the English took it over. Even in 1728, it was a cosmopolitan city that blended customs and people from many lands. This was not regarded highly by the rest of New England. "I guess so. Why shouldn't they?"

Blackpoole sniffed loudly. "Because they are not English, as we are! Is that not reason enough?"

Libbeth thrust out her lower lip in disapproval. "I do not believe her story," she declared.

Blackpoole immediately spun around to stare at her in shock. "Think you she misrepresents the presence of Dutch in New York? Have they expelled them, then? Are they coming here?" Blackpoole turned back to Sabrina with an accusing stare. "Are you Dutch yourself?"

Libbeth ignored Blackpoole's phobias. "I care not whether she is Dutch, English, Irish, or Indian. I think she is the maidservant I ordered sent to me. And I believe she is attempting to avoid serving me."

"What? That's ridiculous," said Sabrina, stunned. "I'm not anybody's servant!"

Libbeth pointed an accusing finger at Sabrina. "See, she denies it to our faces!"

Blackpoole threw off his fears of a Dutch invasion and retreated to his stiff posture of authority. "This is a serious charge, girl," he told Sabrina.

"Have you any proof that you are *not* who Mistress Chestler says you are?"

"No . . ." Sabrina faltered. She had no idea how she could explain who she was without getting into more trouble. "But why should you take her word over mine?"

"She is Squire Chestler's daughter," Blackpoole said, as if that should settle the matter then and there. "Have you not heard of him?"

"Uh . . . nope," Sabrina admitted.

"Do you know of the place called Rhode Island Colony?"

"Yes."

"It was founded on a small chunk of land Squire Chestler did not want anymore. He is the wealthiest man in these parts." Blackpoole waved his arms to emphasize this point. "Therefore what he says and, by logical derivation, what his precious only daughter says, is of course true—if you cannot prove otherwise, that is."

Sabrina was caught in a bind. What answer would get her into the least trouble? She wished she could consult with Salem . . . if he was still talking to her. "What if I say I'm not Mistress Chestler's maid?" she asked tentatively.

Blackpoole tapped a bony finger at his forehead, as if consulting a mental catalog. "If you are not her servant, then you are a stranger, without support and thus a vagrant. Branding or stoning is the usual penalty for vagrancy and also the prescribed penalty for avoiding an indenture. Which do you prefer?"

Libbeth was outraged. "I'm her owner!" she fumed. "How dare you threaten to damage my property like that!"

"But she says she *isn't* your property," objected Blackpoole. "That is why I have to punish her." He and Libbeth locked stares like terriers warring over a bone or a rag.

Sabrina was starting to feel rather chewed-upon and didn't like it one bit. "Don't I have a say in this?" she asked.

Without breaking off their staring, both Magister Blackpoole and Mistress Chestler barked "No!" in unison.

Libbeth had a trump card to play. "Magister," she said smoothly, "do I not recall that you purchased your office with aid of a loan that my father generously provided? Have you earned enough to pay him back? You of all persons should know the penalties for defaulting on a debt." She poured honey on top of the nettles. "You do desire to travel on to England someday and actually acquire a legal degree, do you not?"

Blackpoole swallowed this a bit slower than his stew. Finally he whirled on Sabrina and said sternly, "Since you attempted to avoid your indenture, I should brand or stone you, or, since you are now going to submit to said indenture, which you tried to avoid, I should reduce the sentence to overheating or stoning by pebbles. But out of respect for Mistress Chestler, I shall let you pass with but a warning." He summoned his sternest look and then bellowed, "Beware!"

He held out his right hand, palm forward, and intoned, "In my capacity as the magistrate of the community of West Bridge, I declare you, Sabrina Spellman, to be, body and mind, never failing of duty, on pain of punishment by"—he racked his brain but failed to remember the appropriate penalty—"I shall look it up later—to be the indentured servant of Mistress Libbeth Chestler for a period of not less than seven years!"

☆

Chapter 7

☆

Sabrina was completely stunned, and she remained stunned during the entire foot journey to Libbeth Chestler's house. She hardly realized that she'd already begun her duties by lugging Libbeth's string-bound bundle of wallpaper squares as well as her own satchel and cat basket.

This was not the way she'd planned on discovering Westbridge's history. But with no idea of how the Möbius Trips clerk was going to arrange her return to 1998, she had no choice but to remain in town, even if she had to play the part of a maidservant.

The Chestler house stood on a small hill overlooking the rest of the town. Although built of timbers, it sat on a stone foundation and boasted a brickwork front, flaunting its wealth over the town below. Its windows were made of the same bull's-eye glass as the Woodcutter's, but the Chestler house boasted a full dozen windows—three times the number at the tavern, which as the meeting hall, was the best the rest of the town could afford.

Like all the other houses, this one had chickens and dogs running around the fenced yard. From the rear of the house, beyond a large vegetable garden, Sabrina could hear—and smell—pigs.

Despite the bright daylight outside, the interior of the house was dim. All walls and cabinetry were whitewashed and accented in bright colors to make the spaces as light as possible, but to Sabrina, used to modern indoor lighting, the place reminded her of a cave. A neat, comfortable cave, but a cave nonetheless.

Following Libbeth through the entryway and up the stairs, Sabrina got a brief glimpse of the hall to the left and the parlor to the right. Both had carpeted floors and contained several pieces of sturdy wooden furniture.

The stairs climbed up and over a huge timber in the center of the house. This summer beam was easily fourteen inches on a side and was cut out of the heart of an oak. It looked strong and it had to be—running the length of the house, it bore the weight of the roof and anchored the entire second floor to the support of the central chimney. Still, it creaked under Sabrina's steps, sending a shiver up her back.

The second floor had wide, sturdy planking and was divided, like the first floor, into two long rooms separated by a double fireplace. The left room, with a window facing the river and the drained lands to the west, evidently belonged to Libbeth. It had a walnut chest of drawers, a pair of chairs, a wash-stand with a porcelain pitcher and bowl, and a large, comfortable-looking bed with a gleaming linen spread. It also had a large male figure at the window.

Libbeth screeched in horror, and the man whirled around, panicked.

"My bed! You have laid your tools upon my Irish linen! Papa will fly into a rage if such valuable cloth has been soiled!"

"A thousand pardons, I beg you," he blurted. Sabrina could see now that he wasn't an adult. He was a teenage boy with an especially buff build filling out his balloon-sleeved shirt and tight leather jerkin. His long white neckcloth looked as if it doubled as a napkin at mealtimes. He snatched up tools from the bedspread at random and threw them down to the floor. "I only set them there a moment ago, while I fitted your windows back in."

After assuring herself that the bedspread was truly unstained, Libbeth softened her manner and oozed up to the strapping boy. "And what marvel of handiwork have you brought me today, my dearest Harvard?" she cooed.

Harvard ducked his head shyly and tugged at his forelock. Unlike Blackpoole, his hair was his own, and it was long, rich, wavy chestnut hair besides.

"You wished for clearer glass," he told Libbeth, "but since the panes are all made by spinning molten glass on the end of a pole and then flattening it, there is no clearer glass to be had in West Bridge. So I bethought myself"—and he paused, during which time Sabrina saw his eyes focus with the intensity of the problem he'd set himself—"there must be another way. I thought of the wood I've carved and the metal I've beaten. They are created rough and then smoothed. So I besought myself a fine enough polishing medium—"

"You overwhelm my weak feminine mind," Libbeth simpered. "What, *in brief,* did you do?"

Harvard accepted Libbeth's lack of interest with just a slight disappointment. "I polished out all the ridges in the glass of your window so you might have better light."

Sabrina peered at the glass in the frame. These panes were indeed free of the annoying circles, though they still had a lenslike quality to them that distorted the landscape beyond.

Sabrina's movement attracted Harvard's attention. "I beg your pardon. I did not see that you were receiving a guest," he said to Libbeth.

"She's not a guest; she's my maid—ignore her," Libbeth snapped crossly. "And speaking of receiving, what became of the engraving of the imperial crown that I gave you to copy for my wallpaper?"

Harvard's forehead creased in thought. "The printing on it wasn't in English, was it?"

"No, it was French."

"Oh. Well, the French are dangerous enough." His face cleared.

"What has that to do with my wallpaper not having the proper pattern?" Libbeth motioned for Sabrina to show Harvard the bundle of papers.

The gesture confused Harvard. "Am I not supposed to be ignoring her?" Seeing the thundercloud gathering in Libbeth's face, he rushed to explain. "You see, Magister Blackpoole couldn't read the words under the drawing of the crown, and he said that any words he couldn't read must be dangerous. So he put the paper on trial, convicted it, and sentenced it to be hanged and then burned." Apparently, Sabrina observed, inanimate objects were common subjects for execution in Magister Blackpoole's jurisdiction.

"But why did you carve a baronet's crown?" Libbeth pouted. "That's the lowest possible rank of nobility."

"Oh, that was a kindness by Magister Blackpoole. He lent me an application for baronet rank he hopes to send in one day when he can afford the price. That is the design I copied for the crown. You know I've never seen a real crown. I've never seen anything but this town." He stared moodily out the window to the west. "I yearn to go out and explore wildernesses like the brave souls who founded our town in sixteen seventy-six—where will we again find such spirit as the spirit of 'seventy-six?"

"This is wilderness enough for me, thank you," sniffed Libbeth. "But why would you desire to leave West Bridge? You have a trade—two, in truth, for you are a carpenter *and* a smith. Most men would be envious. Also, you have me. And I know that *all* men envy that as well."

Conflicting answers collided behind Harvard's eyes. After a moment he chose his words carefully. "I would live without envy, if I could. I have two trades only because my uncles could not agree which of their two crafts I should be apprenticed to—carpenter or blacksmith. They settled it by splitting my apprenticeship between them."

"But you are famed the land around for your work."

Harvard sighed. "Because I have the only iron cupboards in New England."

Sidling up to him until she *almost* touched his arm, Libbeth purred, "You can marry me and we'll go to Boston. There you can set up your own silversmith shop. We'll give those Revere boys a race for their money!"

"But would not Boston be much the same as here?" Harvard asked with despair. "The same pinched faces, the same sad lives, the same suit of clothes worn day after day after day without washing." He was flushed with the dream within. "No, I wish to see foreign lands—Susquehanna, Pennsylvania, the Atlantic beaches of New Jersey—*sob.*" His voice cracked, and he turned his face to the corner. "I must leave." Without another word, Harvard picked up his tools from the floor and walked out.

Sabrina broke the awkward silence. "Wow. He's quite a catch."

Libbeth shot her new maidservant an icy glare. "He is not your concern. Mind your place, girl. You have little enough time to spare from your duties, and no time at all for . . . *fishing.*"

"Right," said Sabrina, biting her tongue. "So where is my place, anyway? Where do I put my stuff?" She held out the basket. From inside she could hear a cat methodically shredding wicker.

"You may place your things at the foot of the bed. You will also sleep there."

"Whatever you say. But where will you sleep if I get the bed?"

"*I* sleep in the bed," Libbeth snapped. "*You* sleep at its foot."

Sabrina just looked at her.

"On the floor." Libbeth pointed downward as if explaining the concept to an idiot.

Sabrina laughed. "Get outta here!"

"I most certainly shall not!" Libbeth shrilled, her face red with indignation. "*All* servants sleep where they labor, and your place is at my feet!" She swept regally to the stairwell, turned, and said frostily, "Take a moment to remember your station, girl. Then attend me in the kitchen to commence your duties." She disappeared in a rustle of starched fabric.

"Had enough history yet?" said Salem, poking his head out of the basket. "*I* certainly have. *Ptui!*" He spat slivers of wicker out of his mouth.

Sabrina spun in a slow circle, taking in her surroundings as if suddenly realizing just how rotten her visit was going to be. "This is nothing like they show on TV. History paper or no history paper, I'm for leaving now!" With that she marched to the door. And stopped. "Okay, how do we get home?"

"Umm . . . we have a small problem with that. We can't leave until the agency brings us back. It's a union spell."

"Do you mean to tell me," Sabrina said in a low voice, "that I get to slave and toil for two days while you *nap* the time away?"

Salem gave a little cat shrug. "I know it's tough, but we each have to do what we're best at."

"Sabrina!" barked a stern voice from downstairs. "Come here this instant or I shall have you whipped!"

Sabrina cringed at the thought. "Can she do that?"

" 'Fraid so."

Sabrina pondered this for a minute. Then her jaw stiffened, and her lower lip stuck out and set in a grim line. "No way will I let that spoiled brat have *that* satisfaction. We'll see who outlasts who around here!"

"Sabrina!"

The new Chestler maidservant scooped up her cat and ran downstairs.

Chapter 8

☆

☆

Libbeth waited impatiently at the foot of the stairs to scold Sabrina, but her lecture died on her lips at the sight of the furry black bundle in her maidservant's arms. "Where did that . . . *creature* come from?" she demanded.

"He's mine," said Sabrina.

Libbeth's eyes narrowed. "When I requested a servant, I did not order vermin as well. Get rid of it."

The creature in question flexed a single angry foreclaw into Sabrina's arm. Stifling a yelp, Sabrina quickly scratched under Salem's chin, trying to calm him down. "First of all, he's a him, not an it," she corrected. The claw relaxed. "Second, he's my companion, and I'm not getting rid of him." Her defiant words made Libbeth's eyes narrow further until they were hateful little slits. Desperate, Sabrina added, "And he's good at catching mice."

That idea caught Libbeth's fancy. She cocked her head, and Sabrina could almost hear the little gears turning. "True," came the thoughtful conclusion. "As such it could be considered that I then own *two* servants, not one. And without spending a single pence extra." She drew herself up to full height, pleased with her own cleverness. "Very well, it may stay. But I will not feed it. Shut it up in the root cellar and let it eat mice."

Salem squirmed in protest, but Sabrina gripped him tighter and shot him a dirty look. Then she followed Libbeth through the hall side of the house toward the kitchen. As they traveled, Libbeth offered a running lecture on Sabrina's duties.

"You shall rise at first cockcrow, stir the embers, and build a new fire in my chamber. Proceed to the kitchen where Cook shall have my meal ready. Bring me my food and drink, first awakening me with a soft and gentle cooing, as of a dove. Then you may take my chamber pot and empty it while I break my fast."

Chamber pot? Sabrina hadn't given any thought to the fact that indoor plumbing had yet to be invented. Despite that rather gross reality, she tried to maintain a sense of adventure about it all, pointedly ignoring Salem's wicked cat grin. "Sounds like oodles of fun. And speaking of breaking fasts and all that, do you have anything to eat? I feel as if I haven't eaten in centuries."

Libbeth halted in her tracks and regarded Sabrina as if allowing a hungry person to eat were an entirely new idea in her universe. "I suppose Papa would say, 'If you own it, Libbeth, you have to feed it.'" She turned and sailed onward to the kitchen. "Cook will be making dinner. Perhaps she can spare you a scrap."

Cook proved to be a sturdy African woman dressed in an outfit as plain as Sabrina's. She was clearly the mistress of the kitchen, and even Libbeth deferred slightly in dealing with her. "Cook, this is my new servant, Sabrina. She neglected to provide herself with food. What have you for her?"

"There will be no dinner today, as your father sent word that he would not be returning from Smithton until dusk," Cook answered. "He will have his supper hot then. As for now, there is bread baked. Divide a loaf between you. I shall fetch the butter crock from the springhouse." Moving with a heavy, flat-footed stride, she walked out the back door.

"Oh, fie!" grumbled Libbeth. "A cold dinner and a hot supper! Has the world turned upside down?"

"What's the big deal?" Although Sabrina hadn't seen a clock since she came into town, the position of the sun suggested that it was around noon, local time. "Dinner or supper—that's hours from now, isn't it?"

"What nonsense you speak," said Libbeth. "One would think you knew not the difference between dinner and supper."

"There is one?"

"Of course, you ninny. Dinner is the great mea[l] of the day, the crown of leisure, with the whol[e] afternoon from which to recover. Supper is ha[d] cold, so as not to disturb an evening of dancing an[d] flirtation. In Boston, anyway." Libbeth fidgeted a[t] the mention of that beacon of civilization, obviously wishing to be there instead of in this backwa[] ter town. Seeing Sabrina's bewilderment pulled th[e] squire's daughter out of her funk and brought [a] smile to her lips. "You make me laugh with you[r] foolishness. I shall have to take you with m[e] everywhere, to keep me merry."

Forty-eight hours is all you get out of me, snob[.] Then I'm—I mean, you're—*history!* With tha[t] pleasant thought in mind, Sabrina asked, "Well[,] whatever you call the next meal, I'm hungry. An[y] chance of getting a burger?"

Libbeth lifted her brows in puzzlement. "What i[s] a burger?"

"An all-beef patty, relish, pickle, lettuce, an[d] onion, all on a sesame-seed bun."

Libbeth's amusement vanished. "What was tha[t] incantation?" she asked uneasily.

"Just a fast-food menu," Sabrina said offhandedly.

If Libbeth had anything further to say, it was cu[t] short by Cook's return. Carrying a crock of swee[t] butter in one arm and a small bowl in the other, sh[e] told Libbeth, "I brought a dish of milk for the ca[t] as well."

"You would waste milk on a beast? My father would not approve!"

Holding up the bowl as if preparing to throw it back out the door, Cook said, "It is poured already. Would he approve of my tossing it away? Or perhaps you would care to drink it?"

"Eww!" Libbeth squealed, her lip curled in disgust. "Not out of *that!* Let the cat have it, then." Clearly the thought of drinking from a chipped bowl instead of from fine china offended her would-be aristocratic sensibilities. She flounced over to the table and sat down, waiting to be served.

Sabrina caught the self-satisfied smile that flashed across Cook's face while Libbeth's back was turned. Apparently the old servant knew what buttons to press to get things done her way without the spoiled girl's realizing it.

Sabrina let Salem down as Cook put the dish on the floor. He slurped noisily away at the milk, annoying Libbeth and making Sabrina's stomach growl.

The servant put the crock on the table, turned, and took a curious-looking loaf of bread out of a covered iron pot that sat on the hearth. Several slices had been cut from it already, but it seemed to Sabrina that it had been made in that pot. *They bake bread without ovens here?* she wondered.

The bread knife was a blur in Cook's hand as slices leaped off the loaf onto plates in front of Libbeth and Sabrina. An instant later the bread was back in the pot and Cook was setting clay mugs of cider by their hands.

"Do you have any water?"

"Water will sicken you if it is not boiled first," Libbeth said, truly shocked. "Do you wish to die?"

"Squire left a pot of tea," Cook put in. "Cold it may be, but I will fetch it."

"First milk for a cat and now cold tea?" Libbeth was truly scandalized. "I do not understand where you get these outlandish ideas." Her face soured into a sullen pout. "I need not tolerate it, not in my own home!"

Taking her plate and mug, she fled upstairs to her room, leaving Sabrina to stare questioningly at Cook. Cook just shrugged her shoulders, saying, "Meet me outside when you are done." Then she bustled out the back door.

When Sabrina had finished eating, Cook gave her a tour of the service level of the Chestler homestead. Beginning at the kitchen garden, which had some scattered wild roses and an overgrowth of mint competing with more legitimate vegetables, Sabrina hit all the high spots of colonial-era drudgery. Day laborers and outside servants beat laundry with paddles in wooden troughs, mucked out pigsties, split firewood, and hauled water bucket by bucket out of the well. Everybody Sabrina saw looked tired and unhappy.

After her tour, Sabrina returned to the dark confines of the house. As Libbeth's personal servant, she wasn't expected to work with the outside hands but to basically wait on Libbeth hand and foot. Sabrina proved less than adept at this. In trying to anticipate what Libbeth wanted, Sabrina always seemed to do the wrong thing or be in exactly the wrong place. The afternoon wore on in a series of dropped objects, bumped foreheads, and stepped-on toes.

Supper was a complete and utter disaster.

It started when a stocky, pompous man in a travel-stained cape came stalking in the front door to find Sabrina flinging rose petals up the steps. Libbeth had thought it the height of luxury to have a servant scatter flowers in her path.

The newcomer was coughing wetly but broke it off to glare fiercely at Sabrina. He held his arms outstretched and barked, "Cloak!"

Sabrina didn't know if she should curtsy or bow. She settled for bobbing her head and saying brightly, "Welcome, Mr. Cloak."

"Are you mad?" the man roared. "I'm Squire Chestler! This is my house! Come and take my cloak!"

Sabrina turned red from her hairline to her collarbones. She stammered an apology and stumbled forward to take the cape from the squire's shoulders. But while tugging at the heavy wool, she snagged the ribbon of his powdered wig in the clasp. Before she could untangle it, the cloak slipped from her hands and hit the floor, taking the squire's wig with it.

He clapped his hand to his shaved head and

bellowed like a bull. Sabrina lost her cool and ran upstairs, nearly colliding with Libbeth on her way down. She stayed upstairs until Libbeth summoned her down to wait on her at supper.

It was full dark by the time supper was served. Candles were lit in a pair of holders on the table. On a mirror-backed sideboard enough food for a dozen people was heaped upon several serving platters. Squire Chestler coughed and wheezed as Cook laid course after course out before him.

A dozen or more oysters sat on his plate as an appetizer. Within arm's reach a rough arc of platters held piles of roast fowl, cured ham, and what could only be described as boiled pudding. Libbeth and her father took portions of everything, but barely made a dent in the bounty. Sabrina was sent back and forth to the kitchen to fetch more delicacies, like pickled duck eggs, as Cook chose to present them.

At first she thought the feast to be a terrible waste of food. But when she saw the platters that were removed from the table being passed out back, she realized that everyone else in the household fed off the masters' scraps. The apparent excess, when shared among so many, amounted to bare mouthfuls for each.

The dinner conversation didn't cheer her up any. The squire openly glared at her and muttered to his daughter, "I don't like her."

"Oh, Papa! I *must* have my own servant!" Libbeth whined. "You promised to make me a gift of one for my sixteenth birthday!"

"You promised me you would find a *husband* by your sixteenth birthday!" shot back her father. "Where is he?"

"I have my eye on a prospect or two."

"Faugh!" he snorted. "I keep telling you that you should be shopping in Boston. I see no one in this town worth spending your dowry on."

"Not even 'Prentice Kinklin?" cooed Libbeth.

"What?" The squire's disbelief sent him into another bout of coughing. "That ox of a lad? Why should I consider him?"

"Well, he *is* a smith *and* a carpenter."

Her father got a calculating look on his face. "She has a point there," he murmured to himself. "He will inherit from *both* his uncles someday."

"And no one in the town is handsomer."

Squire Chestler looked up sharply at his daughter. "Handsome shall not fill my hand with silver. A smithy and cabinetry—now *there's* a bargain worth your cost." He fell back to his meal, muttering and coughing.

Sabrina would have stayed out of trouble if she hadn't tried to do something about Squire Chestler's incessant coughing. If her powers had been working, she would have been able to banish the cold symptoms with the flick of a finger. As things stood, she decided to make him some herbal tea to soothe his throat. Going outside, she gathered some mint leaves and a few rose hips from the garden. *Rose hips have lots of vitamin C,* she thought to herself as she dropped them in the teapot to steep, *and peppermint oil will help his sinuses.*

She poured the brew into a china cup and took it to the squire. Still absorbed with his calculations of future wealth, he absently sipped the tea.

"Faugh!" he spluttered. "What has she done to the tea? East India's Own, and she's ruined it! Her very first day and she's spoiled good tea! I will not have it! Throw the wretch out!"

Chapter 9

☆

Sabrina slumped down onto a stump outside the Chestlers' front gate, watching the footman trudge back toward the house in the early gloom and trying to ignore Libbeth's exaggerated sobbing coming from the upstairs window. *Oh, this is just great,* Sabrina thought in despair. *What am I supposed to do now? I put up with being treated like a maggot all day long only to get fired for trying to be nice! Now I'm unemployed, my cat's locked under a house, and I'll probably get arrested for vagrancy two hundred fifty-four years before I'm even supposed to be born! And on top of all that, this stupid bodice is killing me!* In frustrated fury she grabbed at her outfit and started tugging and pulling, but it had been tied so tight it refused to budge in any direction. "I feel as if I'm in a sausage suit!" she grumbled.

"I guess you can eliminate 'household domestic' from your career choices," a dry voice commented from behind the stump.

Sabrina spun around to find two golden eyes in a furry black face gazing up at her. "Salem!" she squealed in joy. "You got out!"

"Of course," he replied, preening his whiskers. "There wasn't a lock that could keep me in *before* I became a cat." He held up a forepaw and flexed his claws, admiring them. "And now I have my very own lock picks."

"I wish I could borrow those for five minutes." Sabrina put her elbows on her knees and rested her chin in her hands. "There's a dress on a certain squire's daughter I'd like to rip to shreds."

"Now, now, calm down." Salem sauntered around the tree stump until he stood in front of Sabrina. "Circumstances may have taken a downhill turn, but at least you don't have to follow them for more than a few more hours."

"Maybe so, but what do I do during those few more hours? You can hang out in the wilderness and eat bugs. I have nowhere to go."

Salem's ears flattened. "I do not—I repeat, do *not*—eat bugs. It's bad enough that in our time they taste like floor wax. In this era they taste like . . . well, never mind." Regaining his composure he continued, "Besides, you're wrong about having no place to go."

Sabrina perked up. "I am?"

Salem pointed a paw down the path leading away from the Chestler house.

"The tavern!" she exclaimed.

Since the Chestlers lived on a hill, Sabrina could see most of West Bridge below, if she stood up and found just the right angle through the trees. She couldn't see the tavern, though. "Salem, are you sure a young single girl is allowed in a tavern alone at night?"

"Please." Salem ran his tongue once over his shoulder, smoothing a disheveled patch of fur. "There's no such thing as television, shopping malls, or miniature golf around here. What do you think these people do for fun?"

Hang out in the tavern, Sabrina decided. She scooped up Salem and started down the path leading to town.

The autumn night was comfortably warm, so the doors of the Woodcutter Tavern were still open. Flickering firelight and music, energetic if a little off-key, poured out into the mucky street. As Sabrina and Salem walked up to the wooden entry porch, the cat remarked, "All *right!* A colonial jam session! Who'd have thought this little burg knew how to rock?" He bobbed his head back and forth to the music's beat, the tip of his tail flicking back and forth in the opposite directions. Sabrina thought he looked kind of cute doing that, but the music was hardly rock and roll. The players did capture the same flavor as the garage bands Sabrina sometimes heard in the Westbridge of 1998, though—a driving rhythm, a few sloppy chords here and there, and sheer enthusiasm winning out over the lack of musical skill.

Salem leaped from Sabrina's shoulder to the top of the tavern's sign. "I'll hang out on the roof, away from the dogs, and just groove on the vibes. Dig you later, chick." Still keeping time to the beat, he bebopped out of sight overhead.

Quickly adjusting her mobcap and smoothing her apron down, Sabrina mentally braced herself for what she thought would be something resembling an Old West saloon, like in the movies. As she crossed the threshold, that expectation shattered.

The common room was filled with townspeople sitting at tables and on benches, all tapping their feet, mugs, or spoons to the lively music coming from the six men beside the hearth. Sabrina was surprised to recognize all of the instruments being played—a recorder, a couple of fiddles, a tin whistle, a viola, and a bassoon. She was even more surprised to recognize the bassoon player as Harvard Kinklin.

The brawny young man used his oboelike instrument like a modern bass player, supplying rhythm and bottom for the other instruments. The music they played reminded Sabrina of a cross between a minuet and a folk-dance tune, and the song being played was apparently a popular favorite—when the group finished, the crowd roared its appreciation.

The men hung their instruments up on pegs

behind the serving counter and dispersed to rejoin
their families, all gathered at assorted tables. Serving women hurried to and fro, loading the tables
with steaming platters of food: meat, boiled veg-
gies, hot bread . . . Sabrina's nose twitched, and a
sharp pang in her stomach, followed by a succes-
sion of emphatic gurgles, reminded her that she'd
been ejected from the Chestler house without a
supper of her own.

Two young boys nearly ran her over, shoving
each other aside to reach a cask and fill double
handfuls of mugs first. A flame-haired young woman sped across the room to seize each boy by an ear.
"Jonas! Jordan! Mind your manners! You almost
did this person an injury," Mistress Juniper Kelleigh scolded them before turning and apologizing
to Sabrina. "I crave your pardon on their behalf,
mistress"—she searched her memory—"Spellman, is it? Whom Mistress Chestler claimed as her
maidservant?"

"I'm not a mistress, not as you seem to mean it,"
said Sabrina wryly. "And it seems I'm not a maidservant, either. Squire Chestler fired me and threw
me out during supper."

Juniper's face registered sympathy. "Knowing
Pinchpence Chestler and his daughter, the princess
uncrowned, I can take it that you have not eaten
tonight. Please, you must join us at table."

Sabrina's stomach screamed *yes, yes!* but she felt
uncomfortable infringing on the young woman.
"No, really, I don't—"

"If you do not," interrupted Juniper, sensing Sabrina's internal struggle, "you will offend two good men of our town. They have caused this celebration in honor of the raising of their nephew from apprentice to journeyman." She waved a hand toward one corner of the tavern, as if to indicate that nephew, but Sabrina couldn't tell who she meant. "Come, Goody Watkins is broaching a cask of William Williams's fresh-pressed cider."

The smells in the place were growing so thick and luscious that Sabrina realized only then that she'd started to breathe through her mouth, just to control the hunger pangs. Giving Juniper a thankful nod, she allowed herself to be shepherded to a table where three girls and twin boys sat patiently with empty plates for the mugs that Jonas and Jordan, on their best behavior now that an outsider was present, carefully distributed. Sabrina was guided to the seat at the foot of the table, opposite Juniper at its head.

Jordan, whom Sabrina judged to be nine or ten years old, hoisted his drink. A sharp "Manners, young sir!" from Juniper froze him in mid-lift. There was a quick unspoken exchange between Juniper and the boy, with the older girl flicking her eyes from the mug to Sabrina's empty place. Jordan flushed with embarrassment and then shyly offered his mug to Sabrina. Then he bolted from the table to find another mug.

Sabrina waited politely until Jordan returned before sampling her drink. Seven pairs of eyes watched her raise the mug to her lips, allowing their guest the first taste.

Slightly fizzy and much tarter than she was used to, the taste of apple juice exploded in Sabrina's mouth. Overwhelmed by the flavor and her sharpened thirst, she continued drinking until the mug was empty, then lowered it with a deeply satisfied sigh.

The others at the table took this as a sign of approval and lifted their own mugs. The younger ones slurped greedily, while their elder siblings, a couple nearly Juniper's age, sipped theirs delicately. Amid gurgles and gulps, Juniper made introductions.

The children were seated in order of age, beginning at Juniper's right, and she recited their names as if they were one long sentence. "Justina, fourteen; John and James, thirteen; Johanna, twelve; Jonas, eleven; Jordan, ten—the Kelleighs. This is Sabrina Spellman, a traveler and guest in our town."

"Father named us all in honor of good King George," explained Justina.

"But he couldn't spell," blurted young Jordan. "I can read *and* write. George starts with a *G* not a *J.*"

"Hist, Jordan. It is not meet that you criticize Father's shortcomings. That you have better schooling speaks more of your blessings than his lack." Juniper sighed. "Especially since he is gone these five years and may not school your tongue himself."

A brief sadness passed over the table as the Kelleighs thought about their lost parents. Justina patted her oldest sister's hand. "Be not sad, Juniper. You do wonderfully well as head of such an unruly clan."

The implications of this sank into Sabrina's brain. It was her turn to blurt indelicately, "You play mother and father to these six? But you can't be more than sixteen yourself!"

Juniper fixed Sabrina with a calm and very adultlike stare. "Sixteen years is age enough. Life is hard and is often shorter than we would wish. Scarce a family in town has both original parents by the time the eldest child is sixteen. Squire Chestler is a widower and Journeyman Harvard was until today a ward of his uncles. We persevere and do what we must. Is it not the same for you?"

Sabrina pondered this. "I guess you're right. I'm being raised by my aunts since my folks are . . . gone." Although both her father and mother were still among the living, Sabrina's father resided inside her magical book of spells, and she was barred from seeing her mother for a period of two years because, as a young witch in training, her mere gaze would turn her mother into a ball of wax. If it hadn't been for her aunts Hilda and Zelda, Sabrina could have found herself facing the world alone, just like Juniper.

The brief silence at the table was broken by the twins who, seeing the chance to seize control of the conversation, started tossing comments back and forth with practiced abandon, arms gesturing emphatically.

"Tell us stories!" demanded John.

"Did you meet Indians on your journey?" That was James.

"Father used to meet Indians in the forest," John asserted.

"Hist!" Juniper ordered. "Sabrina travels between fine cities—New York and Boston—and would have little interest in our small-town doings."

Sabrina swallowed a bite of warm bread garnished with wonderfully sweet-tasting butter. "Actually, I want to hear about the town," she said carefully. "You might even say that getting stranded here was just the thing I needed. Can you tell me how West Bridge was founded?"

"Juniper knows all about it," Johanna stated proudly. "She has written it down in a book."

Juniper gave Sabrina a modest little nod. " 'Tis but a journal wherein I copy out tales told by the likes of Master Watkins, who plies the ferry across the river and talks with everyone, or the Kinklin brothers, Stanford and Berkeley, whose family was among the first to settle here." She indicated two husky men standing next to the counter, flanking Harvard Kinklin.

There was a strong family resemblance between the nephew and uncles. All three were taller than the average townsman, with thick hair that hung in a lazy forelock over well-sculpted faces. The two uncles laughed loudly and thumped Harvard on the back. Then Stanford stepped forward and hooted loudly to get the room's attention. "Good neighbors, dear friends, and *future customers!"* he began, to friendly laughter. "It is with the greatest pleasure and sense of accomplishment that we ask you to join us in celebrating this important day in the life of our nephew, Harvard Kinklin. Sad as it was that he was left in our care by the passing of his father, our eldest brother, Cambridge—"

"And sad as it was that Harvard could not distinguish the superiority of smithcraft over iron-thumping," put in Berkeley who, Sabrina immediately surmised, owned the smithing business.

"—we were most pleased that our young stalwart apprenticed to *both* our crafts," finished Stanford. "He pursued them with the same practical energy and willing mind and indeed surpassed our expectations for any two of our apprentices."

The brothers lifted their mugs, and Stanford said, "Accept our meat and raise your mugs as we present to you Harvard Kinklin, yesterday 'prentice—today journeyman!"

The crowd roared its approval of the speech and of young Harvard, and the celebration began in earnest. Surging forward with platters and trenchers in hand, the townspeople converged on the tavern keepers and their servants, who hustled about, carving and ladling. As at Squire Chestler's supper, Sabrina saw that roasted meats made up the bulk of the townsfolk's delicacies. The centerpiece consisted of a huge joint of beef flanked by two whole roast pigs. A double ring of roast fowl—which looked suspiciously like pigeons, pheasants, or other game birds rather than chicken—made a ramp up to the larger roasts. Sabrina had never in her life seen so much meat heaped up for one meal.

All of the vegetables of choice appeared to be roots—turnips were the only ones Sabrina recognized—and they'd been boiled to a pulp at that. The birds and the pigs were stuffed with minced bread, onions, and savory herbs. *There's no such thing as a salad bar around here,* Sabrina thought, realizing that this kind of heavy food was a must for hardworking people who could burn it off in a day's labor.

Every dish was accompanied by mountains of bread. Sometimes slabs were used as a liner on wooden plates, which she learned were called trenchers, and later savored for the soaked-up juices. The rest was freely torn into chunks and dunked in crocks of salted butter.

Sabrina was surprised by the unexpected pleasure she felt at being part of this rustic pioneer free-for-all. She obtained her share of food along with the Kelleigh clan. Then they all returned to their table after making sure to get refills of cider. Other townsfolk preferred the small beer or stronger brews. Once she sat back down, Sabrina's attention narrowed to the exquisite delight of filling up on good food after a long hunger.

After the relative silence of intense eating, conversation started up again, led by the head table where Stanford and Berkeley regaled Harvard with funny tales of the three brothers' misadventures growing up in West Bridge. Soon after, Master Watkins, the innkeeper's husband and local ferryman, toured the tables offering tidbits and pointed jests.

When he brought his pewter serving tray to the Kelleigh table, Mistress Juniper pulled at his sleeve. "Our visitor wishes to hear tales of our town, and most especially of its founding on the river. Will you entertain her?"

"Indeed," Watkins said, putting his tray down and rubbing his hands together with relish. "As it is my river—"

"You charge as much as if you owned it!" hooted a patron nearby.

"—and the river was the reason for our founding, I shall be happy to tell," finished Watkins with a wink. Taking mental notes for her history paper, Sabrina chewed her food and listened.

"Two generations ago," Watkins said, "a small group of Bostonians grew dissatisfied with the manner in which their town was run. They had come to these American shores in search of perfect freedom and found only new masters and new laws equally as stifling as those they'd left behind in England. They agreed that they should set out west to establish a new town wherein they could live in complete equality. Alas, it was the last thing they ever completely agreed upon."

Laughter rang through the tavern. The tale was obviously popular, and the listeners knew where it was going.

"They set out from Boston, stopping each night to debate which direction to go next. After two weeks' time they had made twenty miles and were in danger of running short of supplies. They determined to elect a temporary leader to guide their journey. Hezekiah Collins was chosen, having received two votes—his own and his son's—all of the others having voted for themselves."

Sabrina couldn't help but grin at the mental image of such an absurd election. Watkins continued his tale with more energy than before.

"Well now, Collins led the party inland, making much better progress by going to sleep as soon as they stopped for the evening. The rest of them continued to debate well into the night, but Collins awoke refreshed each morning and led them on, ignoring all their advice and any arguments to the contrary. Each day, however, the party demanded to know if they had reached West yet. Collins found his dear friends and companions to be a sore trial indeed.

"When at last they reached a river and found a large swamp on the farther bank, Collins declared that spot to be West, and the town was founded. At first the settlement was called West, and the river the same, but when the river had been spanned by a ferry and the swamp drained for farmland, the town's name was changed to reflect this. It was henceforth called West Ferry, being the ferry over the river West. There is now a plan afoot to bridge the river with a covered structure. In anticipation of this, we have learned from our past and have already renamed our town West Bridge."

"Wait a minute," said Sabrina. "Won't a bridge cut out all your ferry business? How can you be so calm about it?"

A sly twinkle lit Watkins's eye. "It's like this, mistress: a ferryman hauls a load of one person to a score of oxen by poling and hauling on a rope as many times a day as his arms can hold up. It is a hard life." He smiled in self-congratulation. "The bridge is my own idea. When it is built, I shall sit at its gate and collect my fares without ever having to get wet again. 'Twas the best way I could think of to put myself out of business!" Amused by his own cleverness, he let out a hearty "Ho-ho-ho!" like a mall-touring Santa Claus.

Sabrina giggled, as much at Watkins's bizarre laugh as at his story. "What a hoot! I've never heard anything like that in my history cla— Eh, I mean the history *books* I've read in my time."

At the next table, a burly man who had been following the conversation turned to Sabrina and said, "There are many who wish their past to be grand, glorious, and planned."

"That miser up the hill, for one!" sniped the apple-cheeked woman next to him.

"And they travel great lengths to convince others it was so," the man continued. "But remember, even the grandest rose began by pushing its head out of the mud."

A cold voice interrupted them. Sabrina recognized it as that of Magister Blackpoole. "Loath as I am to spoil your festivities—"

"You've a power in your tongue, Osbert Miller," someone hissed from the back of the room. "You conjured a mud-head and here he appears!" Sabrina was ready to laugh at the joke, but no laughter came forth from the crowd. In fact, all gaiety in the room came to a screeching halt.

Blackpoole glared around but failed to find the author of the "mud-head" remark. "It is my duty to remind you all that wastage of resources—to wit, candles, in this instance—is punishable by a fine. You may continue your revels, but rest assured, you will be assessed for your mirth."

In an instant, all candles in the room were snuffed out. The only light remaining came from the blaze in the hearth. In the gloom, a coin rang as it struck the hardwood floor at Blackpoole's feet. A disguised voice muttered, "A farthing for the mirth of seeing you fall in a privy."

This time Sabrina knew the joke was not intended to elicit laughter. She could almost physically feel the hatred the townspeople felt for Blackpoole and wondered if the magistrate felt it himself.

If he did, he either enjoyed it or didn't care. Again his stern gaze swept the room in an attempt to spot the offender, but now it was too dark even to distinguish faces. With a scowl he bent over, plucked up the coin at his feet, then stalked to the counter to confer with Goody Watkins in low tones.

The evening's mood thoroughly dampened, people gathered themselves and began shuffling out of the tavern. Sabrina watched as Juniper organized her family, making sure all platters and mugs were returned to the serving counter and stacked neatly for the tavern servants to clean before closing up. *They look so happy together,* Sabrina thought, a little envious. *In my time Juniper would just be another high school student, but here she's successfully raising a whole family!* She smiled as she watched little Jordan, who insisted on stacking all the mugs on a single plate and balancing the wobbly stack in one hand.

As Jordan successfully reached the counter, Sabrina caught sight of Blackpoole and Goody Watkins looking her way. Her stomach knotted. *I lucked out and got a free dinner, but I doubt if those two will let me wash dishes for a room.* Her fears increased when Blackpoole stiffened himself into full dignity and started toward her.

She turned back to the table to find Juniper watching the drama intently. Her expression plainly showed that she had no affection for the pompous and self-inflated magistrate. "I think you would be wise to spend the night at our house, should you wish it," she told Sabrina in a quiet voice.

Greatly relieved, Sabrina took Juniper's hand and pressed it warmly between hers. "I would love to," she replied. "I don't even want to think about the alternative."

"Indeed, neither should I," said Juniper. "No poor soul should be left to suffer what Magister Blackpoole thinks of as justice." Still holding Sabrina's hand, she led the blond teenager out of the tavern, pointedly ignoring the stony gaze of the lanky magistrate.

Salem on Trial

☆

Chapter 10

☆

The waning moon peered over the eastern trees, shedding enough cool light to allow the Kelleigh clan to troop back to their house with a minimum of stumbling. Home proved to be a sturdy but unpainted two-story building closer to the river than to the center of town. As soon as Juniper opened the door, Jordan sped inside to light a straw from the embers of the fire. Cupping it in his hand, he carefully lit a candle that rested on the broad oaken mantel.

In the pale yellow light of the tallow candle Sabrina saw a neat but nearly bare room with chairs hung up on pegs along the walls and several planks laid across sawhorselike supports to make a table in the center. The day's work had been cleared from the table before the family went to the tavern, so the room was half prepared for night already.

With a minimum of fuss and the efficiency of regular practice, the children swarmed through the house, each tackling a specific duty. The boys took the table apart, rearranging the planks and supports to make benches clustered around the fireplace. The girls raced upstairs and pulled blankets and pillows from chests, distributing the boys' share downstairs and arranging their own on the floor upstairs. *They literally "make" their beds!* Sabrina marveled.

Juniper lit a second candle and crossed the room to open the door to an attached room at the back. "I regret we have no proper bed to offer you, as the tavern would," she told Sabrina. "The boys sleep down here and my sisters and I occupy the floor upstairs. But there is a bench you may use in the kitchen, where I trust you may pass the night in warmth and privacy."

Sabrina followed her hostess into the kitchen, which proved to be the only part of the Kelleigh house built of brick. "Kitchens are prone to fire, as you well know," Juniper commented as she dragged a bench to a spot in front of the hearth. "But the embers are well-banked enough to keep you warm if you mind your skirts."

Like a genie, the youngest girl, Johanna, appeared at Juniper's right hand, offering a patched but serviceable comforter and a bolster pillow. "I made them myself, of scraps I saved from the pulp mill," she said shyly.

"They'll make me warmer just knowing that," Sabrina told her. The girl blushed and ran from the room.

Juniper smiled at Sabrina's kindness. "Sleep in peace, for tonight, at least." Taking the candle, she left the kitchen, latching the door behind her.

Sabrina arranged the pillow and comforter on the bench and sat down. Moonlight speared in through gaps in the window shutters, giving just enough illumination for her to see that the room was lined with shelves bearing crockery and boxes. A dim glow reddened the hearth.

"Not exactly the Hilton, is it?" Salem asked from the shadows.

Sabrina re-swallowed her heart before answering the ever-annoying cat. "They're so kind to offer it that I'll enjoy it better than a night in a palace."

"I'll take central heating any day," Salem sneered. "I hate getting my fur singed." He jumped onto the bench into a shaft of moonlight and blinked up at her, the human intelligence in his golden cat eyes sending a little shiver through Sabrina's body. Between those eyes and the ghostly silver light on his shiny black fur, Salem really did look like a magical creature. But only for a moment. When he plunked himself down and began to lick his belly, all sense of mystery vanished.

"I'm sorry I didn't bring you any scraps from dinner, Salem," Sabrina said.

"Don't worry about it," Salem said between licks. "I found a way into the tavern's smokehouse. I ate enough trout to make me grow scales." He belched, and Sabrina caught a pungent whiff.

"Eww—fish breath! Just for that, you sleep *under* the bench."

Salem straightened up, satisfied with the cleanliness of his belly for the moment. "I'll sleep on the mantel, thank you. I've seen washcloths thicker than that comforter."

Sabrina ignored the cat's snobbishness, running her hands along the comforter in the dark instead. Her fingers traced out the seams along the patches. Their stitching felt as tight and precise as a sewing machine's. She thought of Libbeth's fine linen bedspread. "I don't understand it," she murmured.

"Don't understand what?" asked Salem with a yawn.

"Why Juniper, who has a huge family and has practically nothing, can be so sweet and generous, while Libbeth, who has the best that money can buy, is perfectly horrid."

"If there's anything that's constant throughout time, it's stuff like that," said Salem. "And speaking of time, how do you plan on spending the rest of yours here?"

Sabrina had been brooding over that very question all evening. She groped for an answer. "Libbeth and her father made me feel so stupid today. I felt like I couldn't do anything right."

"Well, it's not like you owe them anything. They practically tried to enslave you."

"But I feel that I owe the Kelleighs for all the kindness they've shown me."

"And your point is . . . ?"

Sudden resolve filled Sabrina. "I'm supposed to be here to learn things. I'm going to spend tomorrow doing everything I can to help Juniper and her family, no matter what chores they need done. It's the least I can do for them."

"If that's your idea of 'the least you can do,' you'd make a rotten cat."

Sabrina pushed Salem off the bench. "Enjoy your mantel, brat."

The sun was barely up when foot-scuffling and whispers woke Sabrina on her bench. Prying apart her gummy eyes she saw Justina and Johanna tiptoeing around the kitchen, trying to make up the fire without waking her. Sabrina yawned and smiled at them, shrugging herself up from the bench.

With more of that crisp efficiency, in no time at all a cauldron of porridge bubbled over the fire on an iron hook and a smaller pot on a trivet warmed weak tea. Breakfast at the Kelleighs' was accompanied by much good-natured teasing and chatter about inconsequential things.

Sabrina was welcomed into the conversation whenever she chose to speak, but no one violated

er privacy or pushed discussion further than she
wished to go.

As at the Chestler house, the meal served more
than just the family. Even with eight hungry bellies
to fill, enough porridge was left over in the cauldron to scrape out and slop to the pigs that were
penned behind the house. Sabrina saw eggs being
brought in from the hen coop, but Justin informed
her that they never ate those; they traded them for
things they needed in town.

Sabrina cornered Mistress Juniper as she was
scrubbing out the porridge cauldron. "Let me do
that for you," she said. "I want to work for my
keep."

"Do you, now?" replied Juniper, a subtle question in her voice.

Just then a heavy fist pounded on the front door.
Juniper went to answer it, with Sabrina trailing
behind. The fist proved to belong to the footman
from the Chestler place, who threw Sabrina's travel
chest down on the Kelleigh doorstep. Behind him
stood Libbeth Chestler and Magister Blackpoole.

Libbeth spoke more for the magistrate's benefit
than for Sabrina's. "Let it be known to all that
Sabrina Spellman, being an unsatisfactory servant,
has been discharged from my service. I renounce
her contract and will seek a refund from the
indenture agent." She looked slowly from Blackpoole to Sabrina. "I repeat again, the Spellman girl
is not in my employ. She is, in short, a vagrant."

Blackpoole's eyes glittered as he stepped forward to seize Sabrina by the hand.

"Mistress Spellman is not a vagrant," Juniper said in a calm voice. "She has just this morning entered my employ."

Blackpoole hissed like a snake, furious at Mistress Kelleigh's intervention. He was not a man who suffered contradiction well. His withering gaze swept across the three women, expressing more venom than words could have conveyed. Then he stalked away.

Libbeth sniffed and wheeled about, then marched off.

"Thank you," Sabrina told Juniper. "I really will work hard for you."

"I'd expect no less," she replied.

The rest of that morning was spent on a crash course in papermaking. Juniper's father had brought the trade over from Ireland and had set up an entire plant on his property. He had taught his children the craft, and they all worked together like a well-oiled machine.

In a stuffy shed attached to the house Juniper showed Sabrina her pride and joy—a screw-threaded hand press. It took the two eldest sisters or all three boys to make a print by throwing all their weight on the handles of the press, but long practice had enabled them to make up to a hundred impressions in a day—far faster than they could make paper, in fact.

A few backward turns of the screw lifted the press off the paper. Carefully tugging at a corner, Juniper peeled the sheet back from the block to reveal a repeated pattern of stylized pinecones in pale rose ink. "The block was carved by Journeyman Kinklin, but the choice of color is mine. I must send him several sheets of it today for his approval. Perhaps you will be so kind as to take it to him."

Sabrina was amazed that Juniper would *ask* an employee to run a delivery. Though never less than self-assured, the young mistress seemed to invite cooperation rather than command it.

Her love for her work was obvious, but Juniper became positively radiant when she showed Sabrina her secret treasure. Opening a sturdy chest, she proudly displayed tray after tray of metal type. "It was my father's from before he left the old country. With English rule, there was not much call for Irish printers. When I do not print wallpapers or chest linings, I practice the art of printing. I have a few poor attempts I may show you, in time." Her eyes focused on an invisible future. "I hope one day to carry on his work and print things that everyone will want to read." She fell silent, absorbed in her dream.

The sun was nearly overhead and the raucous clatter of her brothers and sisters gathering for dinner roused Juniper from her fancy. "Enough of daydreams at midday," she said briskly. "I have dinner to prepare, and then you have a delivery to make."

The Kinklin forge sat on the riverbank upstream of West Bridge, where the tumbling waters of the river West ran downhill toward the flatland below. Rather than set up separate shops in the town, the Kinklin ancestors had decided to pool their resources and build a small complex that included work areas for both their carpentry and smithing trades.

Tree trunks split into rough strips fenced an acre or more of land along the hillside, with ditches and flumes diverting river water to several of the buildings within the compound. The flumes were wooden troughs built up on trestles to provide water pressure where they ended over waterwheels. There were two main wheels, one attached to a building, which groaned and rasped with the sound of wood being sawed within, and the other backing onto the forge itself.

The yard bustled with activity as Sabrina picked her way toward the forge. In addition to preparing wood and metal for sale or use in other projects, various townspeople and outlying cottagers brought their own raw materials for rough cutting or refining. Sabrina had to weave her way around oxcarts loaded with various woods that had been seasoned a year or two at small farms and which would now be turned into planks to replace dirt floors. Several other carts bore huge bundles of

firewood for the ever-hungry forge, and their owners were loudly haggling with either the Kinklin
men or their wives about quality and price.

To complicate her progress, the ground beneath
Sabrina's shoes was a churned mess of muck and
manure, as was every other traffic route in town.
Only through careful placement of her feet was she
able to reach the forge without sinking ankle-deep
in unmentionable dirt. The others didn't seem to
mind the mess, either ignoring it or stopping occasionally to rinse their footwear in puddles or
troughs. *Everybody laughs at scenes like this in the
movies,* Sabrina thought, taking a careful step and
then a little hop, as if she were playing some
demented game of hopscotch. *I'd kill for a
sidewalk—or rubber waders!*

The Kinklin forge rang with the clang of metal
upon metal and hissed as hot iron met quenching
water. Even though the building was completely
open on one side, the smoke and the din made it
impossible for Sabrina to see or hear Harvard
inside. She snagged a boy of twelve or so as he
carried newly flattened iron strips out toward a
storage shed.

"Where can I find Harvard Kinklin?" she bellowed over the noise. "I have a paper delivery for
him."

"Not 'ere, mum," the boy shouted back, giving
her a gap-toothed grin. "Master Berkeley sent out t'
fetch load from charcoaler's, out in woods."

In spite of the boy's odd speech, Sabrina got the

gist of the message. "Is there anybody else who could take delivery?"

"'Is order or 'is oncles'?" bellowed the lad.

"I think he ordered it himself."

"Summon else 'on't do, then," the boy declared. "Journeyman 'e is now. 'Is bizness be 'is bizness and nowt else's."

"Can you take it to him?" Sabrina was getting hoarse from all the shouting and the smoke.

"Pardons, mum, but no," he said, shaking his head vigorously. "Got work 'ere, I do—can't go scamperin' off. 'Sides, 'e'll be in a right cross mood t'day—'e forgot 'is dinner, 'e did." He jerked a thumb at a small bundle neatly wrapped in a checkered cloth that sat on a shelf near the door.

Sabrina didn't want to fail at her first errand for Mistress Juniper. It seemed a poor way to do her job, even if she was only going to be working one day. An idea struck her. "Is the charcoaler's near here? Maybe I could take Harvard his lunch and give him the paper at the same time."

"Near enough," yelled the apprentice. "Take Founder Collins's Path out big oak tree way. Foller path. Cain't miss it." That seemed to settle things in his mind, for he and his burden dashed off without another word.

Sabrina considered her options. Everyone in this time period seemed to expect people to do what they had to do, when they had to do it, with a minimum of consultation with others. *I guess you have to be self-sufficient if you're the only people in the middle of a forest. If you don't do what's necessary, who will?* She studied the forge, the muddy street, and the surrounding forest. *On the other hand, this is Westbridge. Not my Westbridge yet, but it will be. I think I can handle a little trip through the suburbs-to-be.*

A half hour later Sabrina was no longer sure about that. She couldn't have been more than a mile or so down the wide rut that she had been told was Squire Collins's Path, but there was nothing except forest in every direction. To be sure, it was a quiet, stately old-growth forest, with clear spaces under the dense green canopy. But there was so *much* of it—and not a sign of human habitation except the path itself. Already she had disturbed great flocks of birds, their whirring wings startling her as they burst from the bushes and fled toward the unseen sky above. And there had been rustlings in the brush, which she hoped were rabbits and deer, not wolves or bears.

Suddenly she realized that the rustlings were keeping pace with her. Something behind and off to her left was slinking through the bushes, stopping now and then, but darting forward through the dead leaves to catch up. Sabrina was no wilderness expert. For all she knew, it could have been a hefty mouse or a light-footed grizzly bear.

Sabrina shifted both of her bundles—Juniper's paper and Harvard's dinner—to her left arm and pointed her right index finger at the spot where the rustling was loudest.

Nothing happened.

Drat! This is no time for a witch to be without her powers! She was going to have to find another way to defend herself. Darting across the path, she spied a length of dead branch that would make for a nice sturdy club. She set down her bundles, snatched the branch up, and hefted it, testing its weight. It was a bit heavy, but two-handed she figured she could whap an attacker pretty good. *All right, whatever you are, let's see how tough you are when your prey is armed!* Weapon in hand, she faced the noise.

"Ooh, aren't you the very picture of pioneer survival," drawled Salem, jumping out of the bushes to balance himself on Juniper's bundle of paper. He sniffed at Harvard's wrapped-up lunch. "Or is it Little Red Riding Hood? I forget which."

"Salem!" Sabrina dropped her club and put her fists on her hips. "What do you think you're doing?"

Salem struck a pose. "No one escapes the uncanny tracking senses of the Wild Cat of the Woods. I know the location of every living thing within a mile."

"This from the cat who can't find his rubber mousie without help."

Salem's tail drooped. "Sneer if you must, but this body has instincts sharpened by ages of time."

"And fattened by too many pouches of Perky Pet Kitty Treats. And speaking of time"—Sabrina pushed Salem off her bundles—"you're making me late. I've got to find Harvard." Bundles in hand, Sabrina turned to go down the path. It curved around a stand of beeches, opening into a sun-filled clearing dominated by a massive oak tree.

Something about the clearing seemed familiar to her, but she couldn't quite put her finger on it. She had followed the forge boy's directions and was sure she hadn't gotten lost. This was where she was supposed to be. But why did she have the feeling that she'd seen this place before? Her quest for Harvard almost forgotten, she walked across the clearing, shifting her view of the tree.

Wait a second! Sabrina gasped. *It's the same tree in our backyard, only smaller!*

The tree didn't have the thickness and the air of great age that she remembered, nor did it bear scars from where a swing had been—or rather *would be* hung—but it had that same division of the trunk into four points. This early in its life, the resemblance to a crown was more striking than in Sabrina's time. The four mini-trunks tapered rapidly as they left the main body and, with their red and gold plumes of autumn leaves, truly looked like some gaudy coronet of nature.

There is something special about it, Sabrina thought. *Some sort of power that can be felt, even by ordinary people. No wonder it wound up with the Spellman house right in front of it. Hilda and Zelda were right—there is a magic in things that grow!* The thought tickled her. *I might even join them in their gardening when I get back.* She imagined her aunts working on their garden, like a ghostly over-lay between her and the real tree. Over there would be the roses, and over there the bird bath, and over there . . .

Up to this point, Sabrina had been thinking of her trip to West Bridge as if it were a visit to a theme park or restoration project. But here, in front of her, was the younger version of something she knew from her own time.

She looked down in awe. *I'm standing where my house will be*—two hundred seventy *years from now!* Her breath quickened in shock, fighting against the tightness of her corset. The world spun around her and went dark.

Chapter 11

A moment later Sabrina found Harvard Kinklin bending over her, rubbing her hands.

"I'm okay," she said, struggling to her feet. "Really I am. I just got dizzy looking at that tree."

"Thirst had stopped me on my way home," Harvard said, pointing at the stream running in a low bed nearby. "You saw me not, but I saw you fall and rushed to give aid."

Sabrina noticed the ox and cart pulled to one side of the path beyond the clearing. Its wide bed was nearly filled with grimy sacks of charcoal. "I came to deliver some paper for Mistress Kelleigh—and your lunch, er, dinner, which you forgot."

Harvard accepted both bundles with pleasure. "Come, ride back with me and we both shall feast."

Harvard helped Sabrina into the cart and climbed aboard himself, taking the reins and clucking the ox into motion. Salem leaped up on the benchboard, settled down between the boy and the girl, and promptly went to sleep.

The squeak of wide, solid cartwheels on un-greased axles pierced the forest as the ox-drawn cart trundled slowly down the path. Moments later the clearing was lost behind them. Sabrina and Harvard rode through the woods, munching on Harvard's lunch.

They laughed and talked for a while, until Harvard said to Sabrina, "You do not think or speak like a servant girl."

"Yes, well, your Mistress Chestler jumped to that conclusion and refuses to think any differently," Sabrina remarked tightly.

"Aye, she is prone to that," Harvard agreed. "She sees only surfaces—refined and sparkling ones at that." He frowned in thought and inner disquiet. "I do not know you, Mistress Spellman, but somehow I have an urge to speak my thoughts to you. It is strange."

Sabrina smiled at him. "Go right ahead. I know somebody sort of like you back home, and I know how much it means to him to have someone to talk to."

Harvard nodded his head at this, but didn't speak for a while. Then he took a deep breath, and the words came tumbling out of his mouth as if he'd never had the opportunity to share his thoughts with anyone before. "I work all day with materials—wood and metal—and I see what ob-

ects are before they become whatever shape we
ammer and carve them into. I look at a chair and I
ee the beech in its glade before we felled it, sawed
t, gouged it, and finally nailed it into something to
upport a rump. And even a nail, to me, rings of the
ammer and the forge, of the smelting works and
ltimately the ring of pick on ore. Everything goes
hrough a process of refinement, from raw nature to
arvesting to transformation by trade, craft, or
tation in life into a polished product. We are, in
ffect, each our own master's piece—that work we
resent to prove that we are now expert in our
rade." He fell silent again for another few yards.

"There are those in the town who would see me
s very nearly a finished piece myself. They would
ave me add a wife and family to make a set, but I
vould be as they see me now for the rest of my
ife." He kept his eyes averted from Sabrina, as if
xpecting her to condemn this.

"That's the way I've heard things were in the old
lays—I mean, these days," Sabrina said, wonder-
ng what was really bothering Harvard.

Emotion crept into his voice. "I wish to roam,
ut I am expected to put down roots. I fear that one
lay I shall wake up to find I have lost the power to
lream." A strange sadness filled his face as he
:oncluded, his voice barely audible, "And worse
et, never having noticed that I had lost it."

Sabrina welcomed the silence that fell after Har-
ard's confession The path curved around a stand
f willows at the edge of a creek trickling toward

the town. To Sabrina, West Bridge looked like civilization's farthest outpost. But seen through Harvard's eyes, it was a pressure cooker of conformity that he feared would squeeze all the wonder and creativity out of him. *Just like high school,* she thought wryly. *No matter where—or when— you are, you want to be someplace else.* The Möbius Trips slogan came back to mind. *No wonder they've made a way for you to travel through time. It's the best way to learn that everybody in every time had the same problems. History isn't dead past; it's today, after you've survived it and moved on.*

She thought of Mrs. Hecht's attempts to get her students to see history as more than just a list of dates and events to be memorized. *Those things were almost by-products of people's lives. Sure, some people set out to do great things, like Squire Chestler wanting to be rich and Libbeth wanting everyone to think she's nobility. She's not much different than my Libby. But the rest of the townspeople are just trying to make ends meet and get through each day. Hey, the town was even founded by mistake, if you want to see it that way. But even if that's true, the accomplishments of the townsfolk are what matter now, and they're what will matter centuries from now as well.*

Sabrina leaned back on the jouncing bench and took another look at the town, still a half mile or so ahead. *I'm ready to write that paper for Mrs. Hecht now. And the funny thing is, I may have trouble keeping the paper* down *to ten pages.* The conclusion filled her with such satisfaction that she broke out into a smile.

But seeing Harvard still troubled by such an unhappy view of his future dimmed her joy. She decided to do something to take his mind off things.

"Hey, want to hear a joke?" she asked.

The question took Harvard by surprise, but like Sabrina's own Harvey, the young man easily shifted gears, putting aside his own feelings to accommodate the new topic. "Do you mean a jest? Certainly."

"Knock-knock."

Harvard just looked at her.

"You're supposed to say 'Who's there?' " Sabrina coached him.

"Oh. Who is there?"

"Interrupting cow."

Harvard laughed. "That is very strange."

"No, that's not the joke yet! I say, 'Interrupting cow' and you're supposed to ask, 'Interrupting cow who?' "

Bewildered but curious now, Harvard obediently said, "Interrupting cow wh—"

"Moo!" Sabrina laughed. "Get it?"

Harvard's bewilderment won out over all possible curiosity. "No."

"Okay, okay, we'll do it again," Sabrina said. "Knock-knock."

"Um . . . who is there?"

"Interrupting cow."

"Interrupting cow wh—"

"Moo!"

Harvard's mouth quirked as he analyzed this new form of humor. Then he erupted into genuine laughter. "I grasp it now. 'Tis quite amusing!"

Sabrina clapped her hands in triumph. Not only had she drawn Harvard out of his unhappy funk, she'd finally found somebody who appreciated a good stupid knock-knock joke! "I've got tons more. Okay, knock-knock!"

"Who is there?"

As the oxcart plodded slowly toward West Bridge, the sound of laughter became louder and louder. By the time the cart reached the Woodcutter Tavern, its two passengers were laughing so hard they didn't notice the crowd of townspeople gathered near the tavern door.

Looking not at all amused, Magistrate Blackpoole and Libbeth Chestler stepped out into the road to block the cart's progress. Libbeth's footman appeared out of the crowd and, without a word, snatched Salem off the jouncing bench, roughly jamming the startled, half-asleep cat into a big iron birdcage. "Hey—" Sabrina began angrily, but Harvard cut her off with one swift motion of his hand. All humor had left his face. Something was up, but Sabrina had no idea what.

Clearing his throat, Blackpoole asked Libbeth

loudly, "Mistress Libbeth Chestler, citizen in good standing of the town of West Bridge, do you recognize this woman?" He pointed at Sabrina.

"I do, Magister Blackpoole," Libbeth answered formally. "And I demand that you seize and imprison her for the crime of witchcraft!"

Salem on Trial

eudly. "Mistress," said Libbeth Eastleigh, "citizen in good standing of the town of ... is hidden. do you recognize of woman?" He pointed at Sabrina.

"I do," Sabrina Blackpoole. Mistress answered grimly. "And I daresay that you stole and ran ... be witchcraft."

☆

Chapter 12

☆

Salem!" Sabrina tried to snatch the cat-crammed birdcage away from Libbeth's footman, but the man stepped out of reach. Salem, fully awake now, hissed but thankfully knew better than to speak.

Harvard leaped down from the oxcart, using his own body to shield Sabrina from Libbeth and Blackpoole. "You make accusations without foundation. What witchery has this woman done?"

"Stand aside, Journeyman Kinklin," Blackpoole ordered. "As one of her victims, it is only natural that you are unaware of her offenses."

Libbeth pressed herself against Harvard, doing, in Sabrina's opinion, an overblown Scarlett O'Hara routine more than two centuries before it was destined to become a cliché. "Oh, Harvard, my dearest, soon we shall have you freed of this vile witch's spell, and as soon as you have returned to your proper self, we shall be married and set off for our new life in Boston."

Harvard's response came with surprising calm and assurance. "But I am under no spell. And I do not think I have any desire to remove myself to Boston. If I were to go anywhere, it would be to the uttermost West—Ohio."

"That you wish to flee your own people and forsake your betrothed and do not think you are bewitched is the clearest sign that you are bewitched indeed!" accused Blackpoole ominously. "Now stand aside, for we must take the witch Sabrina—a Dutch name if I ever heard one—inside to her trial, which is already in progress."

"What?" Sabrina gathered up her skirts and hopped down from the oxcart. The gathered crowd gasped at such an unladylike move and stepped back en masse, as if afraid of the girl. "Hold on there!" Sabrina snapped, narrowing in on Blackpoole. "How can you put me on trial for something I haven't done *and* start it without me?"

Blackpoole ushered Sabrina into the tavern with little shooing motions. "Crime is crime, and accusation of a crime is all that is needed to begin a trial. In your case, since the crime of witchcraft is indefensible, it is not necessary for you to be present during the prosecution. And since the sentence is invariably death by some awful but just means, your presence is needed only for your execution." He snatched the iron cage containing

Salem from the footman's hand. "Totally logical and completely legal."

Salem growled, his golden eyes narrowed to slits that pierced Blackpoole with a scornful glare. Sabrina could only guess at what he would have told the magistrate if he could have used his voice at that moment.

Ignoring his unusual captive, Blackpoole strode into the tavern. The crowd pushed Sabrina in after him.

The first time Sabrina had gone from the bright sunlight into the tavern's gloom it had felt like a simple step into a building. This time the same transition felt like falling into a nightmare from the Dark Ages. The perpetual fire in the hearth was less a symbol of coziness and welcome than a threat of ignorance, anger, and torment.

Libbeth dogged Sabrina's heels as Blackpoole stalked through the empty tavern to take a place behind the counter. With a jarring thump he set Salem's cage down, produced a gavel from his pocket, and rapped sharply on the counter. "The trial of Sabrina Spellman, witch, has commenced! We pronounce the accused guilty! Now, moving to the penalty phase . . ."

Sabrina's stunned outrage was no match for Libbeth's. Her cry of "But I didn't do anything!" was drowned out by Libbeth's "But I haven't given my testimony yet!"

Blackpoole's face pruned in frustration. "I see no

need for extending the duration of this case, Mistress Chestler."

"Then my father will see no need for extending the duration of your loan," Libbeth snapped back.

Blackpoole's gavel wavered as he weighed his zeal to impose a penalty—any penalty—against the horrible threat brandished by this fiend in the guise of an innocent young woman. He was also uncomfortably aware of the crowd in the tavern, who might take action against *him* if they were cheated out of a spectacle. West Bridge was a small community, and a witch trial would keep the firesides lively throughout the long, cold winter. This was no small matter. This trial could make or break Blackpoole's reputation.

"Let us convene court, then, that we may hear your evidence of the witch's crimes!" he decided.

The townspeople eagerly arranged themselves at the tables and benches of the tavern, with Goody Watkins circulating among them, taking drink and food orders. Magister Blackpoole dragged a battered chest out from under the counter, which produced a musty black jurist's robe and a stack of heavy law books. The books went on the counter next to the gavel, while the robe was hung over Blackpoole's bony frame. "Magister Blackpoole, prosecutor and judge by power of the Crown, present and presiding," he intoned.

Libbeth stood impatiently next to the counter while her footman brought first one chair, then a second and a third for her inspection. Five chairs later, Libbeth found one to her liking and, fluffing her skirts to full effect, sat down majestically to give her testimony. "Mistress Libbeth Chestler, plaintiff, witness, and sorely aggrieved victim, present and accusing," she said primly.

The crowd murmured its approval.

Sabrina, meanwhile, stood dumbstruck in front of the counter where the footman had left her. Poor Salem couldn't help her, and indeed he was just sitting in his cage helplessly watching the proceedings. Sabrina was going to have to rely on her own wits here. "Don't I get a defense attorney?" she wailed.

"Witchcraft is indefensible," Blackpoole stated flatly. "And who would risk his reputation and the accusation of complicity in witchcraft to defend a witch?"

"I would!" a clear, confident voice spoke up from the crowd. Surrounded by her brothers and sisters, Mistress Juniper Kelleigh stood up and stared defiantly at Magister Blackpoole.

"Denied!" barked Blackpoole.

"And why may I not?" Juniper demanded.

"You have no standing before this court."

"Nonsense," snapped Juniper, her temper flaring. "I am a citizen of good standing. I engage successfully in commerce by papermaking and printing. Have I not paid my taxes and tithes as a proper subject of the Crown? Why should I be denied the opportunity to defend one I believe is spitefully accused and unjustly tried?"

Blackpoole patted the law books before him. "Because, according to custom and law, the only persons with any standing before a court are male owners of property with substantial wealth. You are a mere woman. By constitution and custom, you have not the intellect to reason the way a man would. Additionally, I feel you are tainted by too much education. Too much thinking is distasteful in an unmarried woman."

"I told you to discard those books and take a husband years ago," simpered Libbeth from the stand.

Juniper turned as red as her hair with indignation. But disagree with Blackpoole's words as she might, she could not deny that the law upheld his position. She stood silent, her fists clenched at her sides, giving Sabrina such a look of anguish mixed with fury that Sabrina felt a tingle run up her spine. Then, defeated, Juniper pushed her way through the crowd and stomped out the door, followed by her equally enraged and stomping siblings.

Blackpoole banged his gavel. "Court recorder, let the record show that Mistress Juniper left in objection to the court's wishes and should be charged with contempt after these proceedings are concluded!"

A woman in the crowd timidly raised her hand. "Um . . . Mistress Juniper *is* the court recorder."

"Oh." After a pause, Blackpoole banged his gavel again. "Then let the record show that there will be no record of these proceedings! The prosecution may now present her case."

"Wait! I wish to speak in Sabrina's defense," declared Harvard, stepping forward.

"Do you need more proof of his bewitchment?" Libbeth complained to Blackpoole. "She has enspelled my beloved to risk his life and reputation for a witch!"

The magistrate frowned at Harvard. "If you continue your obstinate defense of this witch, I shall have to appoint you bailiff to the court."

Harvard did a double take. "Huh?"

"Journeyman Harvard Kinklin," Magister Blackpoole boomed, "I hereby appoint you bailiff to the Crown in the service of this court, to maintain order in this chamber and to remove those who disturb the proceedings of this court. Do you swear to uphold the Crown and the laws of England, knowing that to violate this service be tantamount to treason against king and Parliament?"

"I do not understand," Harvard answered, his confused expression showing as much, "but I will match my loyalty and trustworthiness against any other man's."

"Then I confirm you in the office of bailiff," pronounced Blackpoole. "Your first duty shall be to remove from this court a person who is disturbing

his proceeding and obstructing the mechanisms of
ustice. Bailiff, remove yourself!"

Harvard's mouth gaped in shock and surprise.
Slowly he realized how Blackpoole had maneu-
vered him into a position where he could not
defend Sabrina without bringing the full weight of
he law upon himself. Blackpoole was petty and
greedy, but he knew how to use the law to get what
he wanted. Gritting his teeth, Harvard marched
out of the tavern, slamming the door loudly behind
him.

"Now, if we have no further obstructions . . ."
he magistrate said, sweeping the room with a
aserlike stare. Townspeople shifted in their seats
and avoided eye contact. "Then we shall proceed.
Mistress Chestler, present your charges. When did
you first become aware that the accursed, er, *ac-
used* was a witch?"

"Well, Your Honor, besides the fact that she
criminally denied being under legal contract to
serve me, as you are well aware, she attempted to
foully poison my father, the good Squire Chestler."

The spectators oohed gravely at this charge.

"I did not try to poison him!" Sabrina objected.
"I made some herbal tea to soothe her father's
cough!"

"Then you admit to compounding a sorcerous
brew!" Blackpoole cried.

"There was no sorcery involved," Sabrina insisted. "It was just some mint and rose hips from

his own garden. An old wives' remedy. My aunt
make it all the time!"

"Are these aunts of whom you speak old? A
they wives?"

Sabrina hesitated. Zelda and Hilda Spellma
were old—hundreds of years old, as a matter o
fact—but she didn't think saying so would help h
case. "Let's call them *mature,* and no, they aren
married."

Blackpoole banged his gavel. "Let the recor
show that the witch admits to having learned h
arts from aged unmarried crones—known by the
very nature to be suspect as witches themselves—
and to practicing those arts upon the body of th
richest, most important citizen of our town."

The idiocy of the man made Sabrina want t
scream. Not only was he as just and honorable as
snake oil salesman but he kept ordering notes to b
taken by a court recorder who wasn't there! "That
not witchcraft," she said in defense of hersel
"that's medicine!"

"Same thing, if one is not a physician licensed b
the Crown after payment of the appropriate fees,
Blackpoole countered smoothly. "Let the recor
show that the witch never applied to myself, a
representative of the Crown, for such a license an
paid me no fees. Additionally, I must warn th
witch once again of the severe penalties chargeab
against anyone who defends a witch, even herself.

Blackpoole's logic, or lack thereof, mad
Sabrina's head spin. "If you're trying to condem

me as a witch, how can defending myself make it any worse for me?"

Apparently Blackpoole's unique brand of logic challenged even him, because he had to pause and think about Sabrina's remark until his face paled with the effort. He narrowly escaped an endless logic loop by vigorously shaking his head and plastering a stern expression over his frown of confusion. "It certainly makes it worse for me, having to find a proper punishment for each of your crimes and then determining which takes precedence and to what degree," he told her as if this were some incredibly wise deduction. "It certainly would not do to have you put to death before all of the sentences were carried out, especially when some of the penalties are also punishable by death. Being already dead is not an acceptable way of avoiding being put to death." With that said, he gestured to Libbeth. "Continue, Mistress Chestler."

Libbeth pointed dramatically at the accused. "I also charge that Sabrina the witch did use unnatural means to alienate the affections between myself and my property—I mean, my properly intended husband-to-be, Journeyman Kinklin."

"I didn't do anything to Harvard," said Sabrina. "Hey, I've already got a boyfriend of my own."

"Do you deny traveling in the forest with Journeyman Kinklin without benefit of chaperon?" Blackpoole asked.

"I delivered some paper to him and took him his

lunch," Sabrina explained. "He gave me a ride back to town in his cart, and I told him knock-knock jokes."

"Let the record show that, as is common with witches, the witch Sabrina did flout feminine modesty and behavior, both with the town as a whole and with Journeyman Kinklin in particular, inciting a solid, sober citizen to scandalous public mirth and mockery."

Her frustration factor was so high now that Sabrina could have pressed license plates with her molars. "This is all nonsense!" she shouted. "You're simply twisting meanings! Everything I'm being accused of is based on the charges of a rich snob who has her nose out of joint because she didn't get everything the way she expected it to be!"

The crowd rumbled a grudging approval at this. Not a few of them had suffered from Libbeth's temper in the past, and her overbearing ways had won her no friends in town.

Sabrina tried to whip this small resentment into a force to counter the railroading that Libbeth and Blackpoole were inflicting on her. "I challenge this self-appointed and self-serving court to present even *one shred* of physical evidence that there was any witchcraft that could in any imaginable way be connected with me!"

To Sabrina's surprise, Libbeth signaled her footman with a wave, and the servant unfurled a gleaming linen bedspread, draping it over the counter in front of Blackpoole. Sabrina recognized the spread as the one she had seen on Libbeth's bed, but she didn't recognize the blurry-edged brown and black streaks that ran across it in parallel lines.

"Behold my bedcover," announced Libbeth, nearly in tears. "The finest Irish linen, imported by my father at immense cost and intended to grace my wedding bed after I had married. See how it bears the marks of burning—a burning done by no implement known to man. A sorcerous burning committed by the witch Sabrina as revenge against me for my father having justly cast her out from his house!"

The crowd had supported Sabrina's accusation that Libbeth was a brat, but the linen puzzled and even frightened them. Sabrina herself was puzzled, wondering what had really happened to the fine material. *Libbeth wouldn't have done that herself, just to condemn me . . . would she?* she wondered.

Libbeth wasn't finished. With a dramatic sweep of her arm, she brought an accusing finger whipping around to point directly at Salem, a pathetic sight indeed stuffed in the iron birdcage sitting on Blackpoole's table. "And here is physical evidence of witchery enough to convict her without a doubt! A black cat, her witch familiar, whom she keeps at her side at all times!"

The evidence was overwhelming. In one voice the crowd cried, "Witch! Witch!"

Magister Blackpoole stretched his hands forth and bellowed in his most official voice, "Sabrina the witch, you stand convicted of the crime of black sorcery! Owing to the complex nature of your crimes, I order you to be imprisoned at once while I study the proper methods and order of punishments appropriate to end your life without mutual conflict. Your final sentence shall be pronounced at tomorrow's dawn, before breakfast.

"Lock her up!"

☆

Chapter 13

☆

A heavy knock resounded through the small brick room with the iron-barred window. A key rasped in the wrought-iron lock, and the bolt slowly, unwillingly slid open.

Sabrina and Salem had been imprisoned in the small room off the main hall of the tavern for several hours. A three-legged stool, with one leg slightly shorter than the others, had been provided for Sabrina to sit on, but Salem was still stuffed in his iron birdcage. A heavy iron padlock had been fastened to the cage's door to prevent the cat from escaping.

To Sabrina's surprise and annoyance, Salem had promptly gone to sleep after their conviction, and he hadn't stirred once since their imprisonment. Goody Watkins had served supper to the crowd immediately after the trial, capitalizing on the

119

extra business, but the tavern had been quiet fo some time since then. Light had entered the room through the barred window until the sun had set and now the cell was both silent and dark.

The heavy wooden door creaked open a few inches, then jammed. Sabrina wasn't sure what wa coming through, so she shrank into the farthes corner and waited.

Someone outside pushed on the door. It budge maybe an inch. Another push, another inch. Who ever it was finally fetched the door a solid kick, an it flew all the way open, smacking into the wall a the end of its wide swing. Startled, Sabrina presse herself farther into the corner, grateful to hav chosen to cower in the one place barely out of th door's path.

A hand holding a lighted candle in a metal holde thrust itself into the room. Then, to Sabrina's grea surprise, Harvard Kinklin poked his head in afte it, suddenly aware that he might have hit Sabrin while forcing the door open. "Pardon," he mut tered, pulling his forelock. "Sometimes I forget m own strength."

"What are you doing here?" Sabrina asked, keep ing her voice to a whisper. "I didn't think anyon would be permitted to visit the condemned, not i Black*foole* had his way."

"The fault is his own," Harvard grinned sel consciously. "It was he who made me bailiff. I too the liberty of arranging dinner to be brought t you."

"Oh, great," sighed Sabrina. "I get the traditional last meal, but I don't even get to put in an order."

"I am sorry if you wished something in particular," said Mistress Juniper, entering the cell bearing a tray covered by a cloth. "I brought the best fare my poor household could supply—Goody Watkins shrank at the idea of feeding a witch."

"How many times must I tell everybody that I'm not . . ." The words froze on Sabrina's lips. To tell the absolute truth, she *was* a witch! But that wasn't something to admit in this time period, even to friends like these. "I can assure you that I did no witchcraft to anyone in town." This was the absolute truth, her powers having been sealed by the Möbius Trips clerk before she was sent back in time.

"Oh, we believe you," said Juniper. "We have lived with Mistress Chestler's spite and Magister Blackpoole's incompetence for many years now."

"There is nothing we can do," added Harvard, setting the candleholder down on the floor, "but to make your final hours less uncomfortable than they might be."

"How thoughtful," said Sabrina, trying mightily to keep the sarcasm out of her voice. Juniper and Harvard were doing all that they could, under the circumstances. After all, Sabrina was a stranger to their world. They were the ones who had to face their fellow townspeople for the rest of their lives. *Of course, that applies to me, too,* she thought. *At least until tomorrow morning!*

Harvard left the room and returned with another stool, which he set in front of the other one, creating a makeshift table for Juniper to set her tray upon. Juniper whisked the cloth away, revealing a plate with half a roast chicken, some boiled vegetables, a mug, and a corked clay bottle of cider.

She reached into the pocket of her apron and brought out a small, thick book, a roll of her best paper, and a handmade box containing a pen and an inkwell. She pressed the items into Sabrina's hands. "It is customary to allow the condemned a chance to pen a final farewell, should they wish it. I would be honored if my humble crafts might give you that ease. As a further solace, I give to you the private fruits of my practice at the press." She patted the book. "This contains a printed copy of my journal of our town's history. You showed such an interest in this place, in its people and their simple voices, that I thought the book might comfort you in your final hours. Please forgive the crude work; I promise you I shall print better in the future."

Before Sabrina could express how touched she was by this gesture, the dark scarecrow figure of Magister Blackpoole appeared in the doorway. He cast a baleful eye at the scene, then rasped, "If I needed further proof of your witchery, I would have it here. How else but by sorcery could you have enticed good citizens to bring you comforts when by rights you should suffer hunger and fear alone until your doom? Leave here at once!" he commanded Sabrina's visitors.

Harvard locked eyes with the magistrate, a hair-breadth away from losing his temper and hitting the man. Blackpoole measured himself against the young man's brawn, shaped and hardened by years at the smithy. He decided that prudence was his best course of action and so offered no further objection when Juniper told Sabrina, "We shall return shortly to fetch the remains of your meal. Please try to eat something, in spite of the circumstances. Justina made the meal for you especially."

Emotion overcame Mistress Juniper, and tears flowed shamelessly down her cheeks. Clutching her apron to her face, she turned and fled the cell. Under Blackpoole's chilly gaze, Harvard pulled the door shut, forcing the magistrate back into the common room and leaving Sabrina alone.

Okay, I'm still doomed, thought Sabrina, *but at least I have light, reading material, and food—even if I don't have an appetite.*

Salem had awakened at the smell of roast chicken. "Oh, goody," he said, yawning. "Dinner at last. Could you pass me some dark meat? I hate the way the only choice in our time is white meat. It's because the birds don't get any exercise, you know."

Sabrina thought she was going to burst a blood vessel. "How can you play finicky eater when we're both going to die in the morning?"

"Well, first of all," said Salem with a yawn, "I'm really hungry. Second, neither of us is going to die—not here, anyway."

"We're not? Why? Do you know something about the future—I mean, the past . . . I mean, *our* future—that I don't?"

Salem fixed Sabrina with that insolent stare that only cats can muster. "My chicken, please?"

In fury Sabrina wrenched the leg off the bird and jammed it between the bars of the cage. Salem hooked it with his claw and tore a dainty strip off, eating it completely before tearing off another.

The young witch had lived with him long enough to know that she had no chance of beating Salem at the patience game. Salem would talk to her again when he was done eating and not before. *Cats!* she thought angrily.

To pass the time, Sabrina examined Juniper's book by the flickering light of the candle. In spite of the papermaker's modesty, the book was cleanly printed and expertly bound, even having a sturdy leather cover. Inside, meticulously set in tiny type, was a collection of stories about West Bridge, each with notes as to who told the tale, what his or her personal history was, and when the story was recorded.

Just the thing I need for my report—if only I could live long enough to write it. She nudged Salem's cage spitefully with her foot. "Hurry up and finish, fleabag. You're driving me nuts!"

With a cat's disdain for public manners, Salem belched and lay back from the remains of the chicken leg. He kept it between his paws, however, batting it idly from one to the other as he licked his chops. "The answer is quite logical, my dear," he drawled. "Nothing's going to happen to us. Oh, I grant that poor excuse for a trial had me going for a while there, but facts are facts—there's no record of any witch trial or executions ever having taken place in Westbridge."

As Salem's words sank in, Sabrina nearly fell off her stool with relief. *Why didn't I think of that? After all, we were just studying this stuff yesterday. No, wait—it was actually this morning.* A sense of dislocation made her brain spin. *It's so weird to think that I've been here almost two days, but back home it's still the same day I left. It feels like weeks since I sat in class and listened to Mrs. Hecht talk about Westbridge and . . .*

Sabrina's panicked "Yeep!" sent Salem scrabbling in his cage in shock. *"What? Where? Who? How?"*

"Salem!" Sabrina shrilled. "My history teacher said that little was known about this period in the town's history! What if there was a trial and an execution and it wasn't recorded?"

Salem let out a tremulous sigh. "Jeez, don't scare me like that. It upsets my digestion." He thrust a paw at the book in Sabrina's hands. "You're being silly. Your friend Juniper's been recording everything about the town and putting it in that journal, right? You even heard her referred to as the court recorder during our trial."

"You mean the Juniper who *left* the trial and wasn't there to record it?" Sabrina pointed out. "The trial that's *already happened* to us but wasn't in the town history for Mrs. Hecht to mention in my history class? What if a witch and a cat were executed and it didn't get recorded?" Blackpoole's obvious distrust of Mistress Juniper and other "overeducated females" flashed through her mind and made her mouth go dry. "Or what if it *did* get recorded, but a certain local magistrate made sure that record got destroyed later—maybe along with the recorder?"

Salem tried to resist the logic in this. Still batting his chicken bone back and forth between his paws, he said, "C'mon, don't get excited. The clerk from Möbius Trips will probably be along any minute to take us home, and we'll all laugh about what a scary ride it all was."

"I hope you're right."

"I *am* right. Sending your clients through time to get bumped off isn't exactly the way to run a profitable travel agency, is it?"

Sabrina had to laugh. "No, I guess not."

"See?" With a luxurious yawn, Salem settled back down. "Nothing to worry about. Enjoy the experience of historical injustice while it lasts."

Watching the cat's belly slowly rise and fall as he drifted off back to sleep, Sabrina tried to follow his advice. But her mind kept nagging at her. "Salem, when you book a time trip for two days, how long does it last?"

Without moving, Salem answered, "Lemme guess . . . two days?"

"Exactly?"

Salem lifted his head. "Forty-eight hours on the nose. The travel agents are very punctual about those things—keeping track of time is their business, after all."

"It never ends early?"

"Of course not! You pay in advance. It would cheat the client if it ended early. Look, why are you asking all these questions?"

"Because—if we got here at about midday yesterday, local time, we're due to be picked up at about midday—*tomorrow!*" Sabrina blanched. "Salem, we'll be goners at dawn! We won't be around to *see* tomorrow midday!"

A sick feeling engulfed Salem. He pushed the chicken leg to the edge of the cage. "Do you want the rest of my chicken? Suddenly I don't have much of an appetite."

"Oh, this is great!" Sabrina said, frantically pacing her little cell. "Just great! What are we going to do, Salem? We have no way to contact the travel clerk! He may have no idea what's happening to us! We've got to do something, but there's nothing we *can* do! So what do we do?"

"We're not going to panic," Salem said sharply. "That never helps."

"Then what does help?" Sabrina asked, mournfully looking at her index finger. "If only I had my powers . . ."

"But you don't, so we'll just have to think of something else."

"Right. Something else." Sabrina resumed pacing, thinking furiously. "Something else, something else, something . . ." She paused. "This is all your fault, you know. You were the one who guaranteed that nothing bad would happen."

Salem looked shocked. *"My* fault? You were the one who didn't want to spend the weekend digging a garden with your aunts!"

If Libby hadn't been flirting with Harvey in class, I never would have had to write a history paper as a punishment in the first place! "I should have stayed home. I might have gotten dirty, but the closest I would have come to *this* mess would be if I'd dug up a bottle or a broken teacup." Unconsciously Sabrina reached for the cider bottle on the tray and drank deeply.

The bottle was halfway back to the tray when Sabrina froze, her eyes fixed on the container. Her mouth fell open. "Salem . . ."

Salem, caught deep in a funk, had his back turned to Sabrina, but his tail twitched once and he answered, "Yeah?"

"The clerk said that everything that's happened in time has already happened, right? So if I, like, wrote my name on this wall and nobody washed it off, then under a coat of paint in the video game room of the Slicery it would still be there. And if, say, Harvey had to strip the paint from that wall to fumigate or something, he'd see my signature 250 years from now, even though I just did it now?"

"You're giving me a headache on top of my stomachache," the cat replied, "but yes, that's how it would work, in principle."

"Then I think I have a way of getting us home without becoming dead."

Salem turned to face Sabrina, his desperation showing in his big round eyes. "You do? What do we have to do? I'm just a kitten! I can't die here! I still have a world to conquer!"

Sabrina unrolled Juniper's writing paper and uncorked the inkwell of the writing kit. "It's my turn to keep you hanging, cat," she said. "If this works, I'll have plenty of time to explain all about it. If it doesn't . . . well, it won't matter anyway."

Cats are notoriously curious beasts, poking and prodding everything in their environment at least once just to figure out *what* things are. The best way to torment a cat is to not let it satisfy its curiosity. For Salem, watching Sabrina scratch away at the paper with the pen without knowing what she was writing nearly drove him mad. When she then carefully dried out the clay bottle with her apron, rolled up the paper and stuffed it inside the bottle, it was like pure torture.

"Turnabout stinks," he muttered to himself, reluctantly settling down to wait.

* * *

The lock clunked, and the heavy wooden doo swung inward, slowly and steadily this time. Ha vard was controlling his strength as he made roon for himself and Mistress Juniper to enter the cel He looked very solemn, and there were tear track down Juniper's cheeks. "We must take back th tray," Harvard said quietly, "and unfortunately the light as well. Magister Blackpoole would con sider it a waste of a candle. I would gladly pay suc a fine, but he would take the light away nonetheles I am truly sorry."

Juniper kept her eyes averted as she gathered u the dinner tray, not commenting on the barel touched food. "You may keep the book with yo for comfort, even though you may not choose t read it," she murmured. "I wish there was more could do for you."

"There *is* one thing you could do for me," sai Sabrina, her voice hushed and secretive.

"Anything," Juniper and Harvard replied i unison.

Sabrina held out the clay bottle. "Put a good cor in this and bury it exactly eighteen inches deep, si feet due south of the middle of the Crown Oak. She pointed to Harvard. "He knows where that is But you must do it *tonight!*"

"Tonight?" exclaimed Harvard.

"Tonight," insisted Sabrina. Seeing their looks c confusion, she added, "Please! You said you woul do anything if you could."

Harvard answered first. "Though I think you well and truly maddened by your fate, I will do as you ask. It is little enough I can do to make amends for the wrong our town has done to you. I do not think I shall tarry here long after, myself."

Juniper had been peering into the bottle and had seen the rolled-up paper. "I see you have written your heart out, as I would have, in your place. If you wish your final thoughts buried in a certain place as a memorial, I, who treasure words upon paper above all else in this world, will see that it is done."

She placed the bottle on the tray. Without another word, she picked up the candle, handed it to Harvard, and backed out of the cell, keeping her brimming eyes fixed on Sabrina.

Harvard tried for an encouraging smile, managing only a twisted grimace before ducking behind the door and manhandling it shut. Darkness filled the cell like a solid thing.

There was a sound of something scrabbling against metal. Sabrina thought of all the vermin that lived under the Slicery—the thought of what might be under these boards made her shudder. Something iron clanked, and a hiss rasped in the cell. "Drat!" said the lock-picking cat as he leaped from the opened cage onto Sabrina's lap. "Broke a nail."

Sabrina hugged him, feeling his warmth and racing heartbeat. "I hope my aunts are right, Salem," she whispered in the blackness. "I hope there is a magic in gardening that's stronger than witchcraft."

Although she never would have expected it, Sabrina went to sleep—in spite of the darkness, in spite of her fears, and in spite of Salem's sharp claws digging into her flesh every time he moved.

She must have been asleep, because the clanking at the window's iron bars woke her up.

"Hist! Hist!" a muffled voice called through the bars.

The only window to the cell pierced the wall a little above Sabrina's height. About as wide as her shoulders, it was blocked by a cross of flattened iron anchored in the bricks of the frame. Beyond the bars, the waning moon had risen high enough to dimly light the trees and buildings of the town.

Sabrina pushed Salem off her lap, dragged the stool to the wall, and cautiously stepped onto it to peer through the window. Swathed in dark clothes, a tall figure and a shorter one pressed up against the tavern wall. "Who's there?" Sabrina whispered.

"Better we call not our names," said a voice that was clearly Harvard Kinklin's. "But trust that we are friends come to aid you."

The shorter figure spoke in Juniper's voice. "Please forgive us for not steeling our hearts earlier. We could not sleep with the weight of your doom upon our consciences. We mean to free you and spirit you out of town before the dawn."

"Did you bury the bottle?" Sabrina asked in a low voice.

Harvard was startled by this. "Did we . . . ? Yes, yes, we most assuredly did." He hefted a length of iron in one hand and waved at Sabrina with the other. "Now stand back that I may pry the bars from the window and set you free."

"That you most certainly will *not* do!" shrilled a different voice from the darkness. "Show your light, Magister Blackpoole, and seize these bewitched fools!"

From out of the shadows opposite the tavern, the shutter of a closed lantern flew open and a beam of candlelight pinned Harvard and Juniper against the tavern wall. "You were wise to warn me that the witch's servants might attempt to release her in the night, Mistress Chestler," grated the magistrate. To the would-be jailbreakers he barked, "Shall you surrender willingly, or need I call out the entire town to hunt you like rats?"

Their desire to see justice for Sabrina was strong, but both Harvard and Juniper were part of the West Bridge community, and the threat of public shame before their neighbors was enough to drain the defiance from them. Sabrina watched helplessly as Blackpoole and Libbeth shepherded her two friends around the corner of the building.

A couple of moments later the door lock gnashed its iron teeth and the oaken door moaned as it opened. Light from the unshuttered lantern stabbed through the cell past Harvard and Juniper as Blackpoole herded them inside. Sabrina didn't move from her position in front of Salem's bird-cage. The cat had scrambled back inside, but Sabrina's legs hid the fact that the lock was missing.

"If you are so desirous of the witch's company," the scowling magistrate snarled to his new prison-ers, "you may join her in both her cell and her fate!"

Libbeth's eyes widened at this. "I do not care what becomes of the scribbler, but I cannot permit you to take my Harvard away from me," she protested.

Blackpoole held his lantern up high, like a bea-con of justice. "Your toy has defied the Crown, custom, and my legally justified will!" he bellowed. "In attempting to aid a witch, he condemned himself to share the witch's doom."

"You shall not destroy him," Libbeth declared, "or I shall have my father revoke your loan at once! You shall be penniless!"

"Faugh!" said Blackpoole. "He may take away what money I have, but magistrate I still shall be, and no evil shall go unpunished while I am the voice of law in this town!"

Libbeth's mind raced, seeking some way to snatch Harvard from the death that Blackpoole intended for him. "If you seek to condemn Har-vard for aiding a witch—then I retract my charges: Sabrina is no witch! I made false accusations against her! She did nothing against my father but serve him clumsily. I claimed that she enspelled

Harvard because he will not surrender his independence and marry me."

Sabrina reeled, only the wall and the press of other bodies in the little cell keeping her from sinking to the floor. *She's admitted that she lied about me! We can clear up this whole stupid mess, and nobody will talk about executing anyone anymore! Yay, we're saved!*

Blackpoole's face clouded with rage. "Then, Mistress Chestler, you have perjured yourself before my court. For that you shall be punished as well, and your father's wealth and high station shall not spare you! In any event, the witch shall not be acquitted simply because you lied. Even you cannot deny that the burns on your linen were made by sorcery. As you said, they were made by no means known to man."

"What burns on what linen?" Harvard demanded to know.

"She's got weird scorch marks on her precious Irish linen," said Sabrina, "and I didn't do it!"

"I certainly did not," Libbeth said. "In truth, they have lain upon my bed clean and beautiful since given me by my good father, but on the very night this"—and she waggled a finger at Sabrina, not sure whether to call her a witch now or not—*"person* left my employ, the linen was marred. What should I think?"

Harvard broke in. "You should think of your new windowpanes, Mistress Chestler. I believe your finery was spoilt by my good intentions."

"You are confessing to witchcraft, Journeyman Kinklin?" hissed Blackpoole in horror. "Is there no end to the taint of black magic in this town? Is West Bridge a nest of hidden witches?"

"It is not magic, but a thing called optics, which the learned Sir Isaac Newton in England has written about," Harvard said defiantly. "When I ground Mistress Chestler's windowpanes to clarify their light, I believe I created what Newton calls lenses. Glass shaped and polished in such a manner can concentrate the sun's heat and cause tinder to burn. 'Twas the afternoon sun shining through the panes that burned that linen—one stripe per lens, I should guess."

"I too have heard of this thing," Juniper added, excited to finally help. "Journals printed in England have traveled to Boston and thence, by reprinting, to here. They explain this phenomenon, a phenomenon of science, they say."

Blackpoole was ready to explode. "Blasphemy! Heresy! Science is a delusion that should be stamped out, along with women who violate their station by reading and presuming to think! You are all accursed by this witch, and I shall see you punished for it! And then I shall burn that press which Mistress Juniper hides, that no one else in this town is poisoned by it! I shall purify this town of magic if it is the last thing I do!"

As if in answer to Blackpoole's threat, a spot on one wall of the cell sparked with a brilliant flash illuminating the room far brighter than any candle could. From the spot, a nimbus of light began to grow. Though mainly green, other colors swirled in the circle, seeming to move back and forth with some depth, until a spinning disc of twisted space interrupted the very fabric of the wall.

In the center of the disc, two tiny silhouettes advanced at unbelievable speed from an infinite distance. An instant later two normal-sized women stepped from the disc into the crowded cell, one holding a familiar clay bottle, now soiled with dirt and age.

"Aunt Zelda! Aunt Hilda!" exclaimed Sabrina, overjoyed. "You got my message and came to rescue us!"

Zelda Spellman flicked a finger, and the native West Bridge townspeople froze in place. Then she turned to Sabrina, her pretty features set in a reluctant frown. "I'm terribly sorry, sweetheart. It's not quite that simple."

Ever the blunt one, Hilda blurted out, "We're here to arrest you."

Chapter 14

✩

✩

"You're *what?*" shrilled Sabrina.

"On what charges?" demanded Salem, jumping up on the stool.

"Arresting you, by order of Drell and the Witches' Council," began Zelda.

"For violating Rule 735: time tampering and endangering the course of history," finished Hilda. "Now that you know, be quiet for a minute while I do this. It's a little tricky."

She pinched her forefingers against her thumbs and then drew them apart. A shimmering line, like a thread of fuzzy light, stretched between her hands. She made a looping motion, and the ends of the line crossed. Then, moving faster than the eye could follow, she wove the ends together in a complex pattern, tugging it tight with a final flourish. When she was done, a ring of fuzzy light hung n midair, tied together with an enormous knot. It ooked sort of like a ring with a macramé jewel. With a snap of her fingers, Hilda expanded the ring until it touched the walls, passing through the occupants' bodies as if they, or it, had no substance at all. As it went on through the wall, Sabrina, with her magical sense, could feel it snug itself around the outside of the tavern before it winked into invisibility.

Hilda panted with the effort the spell had cost her. "It's a forget-me-knot," she wheezed. "A few minutes from now, nobody in town will remember the last couple of days. Real finicky to do right. Ptolemy Ptung-Ptyde used a triple half hitch instead of a double carrack bend in 3277 B.C. and made one so strong that everybody completely forgot where Atlantis was."

Zelda beckoned to Sabrina and Salem. "Now stand clear of these people so we can transport you back home. We have a lot of things to talk about before we go see Drell."

"No, not Drell . . ." Sabrina moaned. He was one of her least favorite people. He was one of *everybody's* least favorite people.

"Hold on a second," announced Salem. "They're coming with us." He indicated the frozen colonists. "I'm invoking Rule 488, and they're necessary to my case."

Hilda put her hands on her hips. "Why are you pulling a 488?"

"Because Sabrina didn't do anything wrong back

here and they put her on trial. And that Neander thal there," and his tail indicated Blackpoole, "pu *me* in a birdcage. I know my rights!"

Sabrina looked helplessly from Zelda to Hilda to Salem. "Why do people always have conversation around me as if I'm not here? What's going on, and what's a 488?"

"Rule 488 states that a witch who is falsely accused has the right to bring his or her accusers to trial before the Witches' Council," explained Zelda carefully. "But there has to be absolute proof that no magic was involved and that the charge was completely false."

"Sabrina *couldn't* have used any magic," Salem said emphatically. "Her powers were sealed by Möbius Trips before we came. The beanpole and the social climber are our accusers. They had their day in court, and now I demand mine!"

"Oh, you're going to get that, whether you want it or not," said Hilda. "Right after we found Sabrina's bottle in the garden, we got a notice in the toaster to take both of you back to Drell to stand trial for a 735."

Salem sniffed in disdain. "I'll match my 488 against Drell's 735 any day. Just let me bring my two accusers and my two witnesses."

"I think we need to head back home and get a few explanations before we go rushing into a show down with Drell," Zelda said, ever the voice of calm in a storm.

"I'm ready!" Salem cried out, fur bristling. "Hades hath no fury like a cat who's been crammed in a birdcage!"

Hilda looked doubtful. "I'm not sure about all this, but I don't want to face a 1299 for interfering with either a 488 or a 735."

"I don't even want to ask what a 1299 is," muttered Sabrina.

Hilda grimaced. "It's really complicated. And long. You're better off not knowing."

"Enough," said Zelda. "We have to get going." She and Hilda linked hands. Each taking a different note, they hummed a chord that made Sabrina's eyes cross. She had a vague impression of either moving toward the disc on the wall or it coming toward her, she wasn't sure which. Then her stomach did a flip-flop and her brain turned inside out, and she was standing in the living room of the Spellman house, circa 1998. Standing around her were her aunts, Salem, and the four townspeople from 1728, still frozen by Zelda's spell.

Hilda pressed both hands to her eyes. "Time travel always gives me a headache. I really *hate* that."

"It has other effects when you're a cat. Excuse me, but I've gotta—" Salem trotted away.

Sabrina felt desperately thirsty after the time shift. Without thinking, she snapped her fingers and one of the Slicery's Gallon Gulp sodas appeared in her hand. She sucked greedily on the straw to rehydrate herself. "Hey, my powers are back!" she exclaimed after draining several inches of soda.

"Of course, silly," said Hilda. "Your trip is over. The sealing wax has dissolved."

"Save the shop talk for later," interrupted Zelda. "I want to know why you took a time trip without telling us."

"I'll tell you in a second," said Sabrina. "But first, could you please unfreeze my friends? They're really nice, and I'm sure this is upsetting them no end."

Zelda had to consider this for a moment before answering. "I suppose so," she said finally. "I guess we'll have to use a forget-me-knot on them later, anyway." She pointed her finger at the four colonists. Immediately they began moving and, in the case of Blackpoole, shouting, "Witchery! Sorcery! Foul black—"

Sabrina jabbed a finger at him. The furious magistrate's mouth continued to move, but sound no longer came out of it. Libbeth held her breath in terror but could not keep her eyes from darting around the room, taking in the unbelievable number of *possessions* in the gorgeous Victorian house.

Harvard put his hands protectively on Juniper's shoulders and only flinched slightly when Sabrina approached them.

"Y-y-you *are* a witch," stammered Juniper.

"Yeah, well, sorry about that," Sabrina said, embarrassed. "And so are my aunts, as you might have guessed by now. But we're really nice people, and I swear I didn't use any magic while I was visiting. I just wanted to learn about my town."

Their eyes stared in disbelief at the houses visible through the front windows. "We are in West Bridge still?" Harvard whispered.

"Yeah, I guess a couple of centuries did change it a bit."

"Hold on a minute, kids." Flashing her big chipmunk smile, Hilda put a hand on Sabrina's shoulder. "Things are going to be tough enough to sort out without setting up time paradoxes. It's better that your friends not know *too* much about the future."

Sabrina gestured toward Blackpoole, who was still yelling silently and shaking his fist at everyone, and Libbeth, who was wandering around in a daze, picking up antique porcelain figures and fingering the upholstery and drapes. "Those two are definitely *not* my friends. What do we do about them?"

Zelda waved her arms in a circle, and a barely audible shudder passed through the house. "There," she said. "I just sealed the house so no mortals can get in or out of it. We'll just leave them here until we settle things with Drell."

As if conjured by the mention of his name, Drell's voice echoed thunderously through the house. "Ladies! You're making me wait! And you *know* how I feel about waiting!"

Hearing the disembodied voice sent Libbeth diving behind the couch in terror. Blackpoole ceased his silent ranting and turned as white as a sheet, while Harvard and Juniper just stood still—maybe a little too still—their eyes so wide that Sabrina was afraid their eyeballs would fall out.

Salem trotted back into the living room. "I'd say that's our exit cue. Are you guys ready?"

"Give me a moment, will you?" Sabrina pleaded with her aunts, taking Juniper's hand. "I'll be right there."

Zelda twisted her mouth to say something sharp, but Hilda put a finger to her sister's lips. Their eyes met. Zelda relaxed, shrugged, and both women turned to climb the stairs, followed closely by Salem.

Sabrina tightened her hand on Juniper's. "I'm really sorry I made a mess. I promise that everything will be fine, though, really. Please don't be afraid. You can't leave the house until we get back, but there's plenty to do here while you wait. You can watch TV . . ." She snapped her fingers and the living room television zapped on. The four colonists gawked at the sight of humans, animals, and whole landscapes trapped inside a small box. "Or read some magazines or make yourself a snack. The house is yours."

She stared at Juniper and Harvard as if she could will them to not freak out. They stared back, trying hard to understand, but they were obviously still in shock.

Hilda's voice floated down the stairs. "C'mon, Sabrina!"

Juniper's fingers twitched. She barely managed to squeeze Sabrina's hand. "I trusted you to guest with me and my family. I trust you now," she said in a small voice.

Harvard put his hand over Juniper's and Sabrina's. "As do I," he murmured. "Go, do what you must. We will wait."

Sabrina raced upstairs to the second-floor landing, gripping the knob of the stair rail to speed up her U-turn to the linen closet. Hilda held the door open long enough for Sabrina to leap inside and then slammed it shut, sending the four of them ten million light-years away to the home of the Witches' Council.

When they opened the door into the Other Realm, they found themselves in a vast Gothic chamber. Sharp-pointed arches leaped up in stone and glass to a ceiling so high it was obscured by darkness and a few clouds. In hundreds of niches et rank above rank into the walls posed statues of Drell in every medium imaginable. There were Drells in togas, in Renaissance robes, in Speedos. There were skating Drells, there were equestrian Drells, and several very popular Elvis Drells— Sabrina counted at least a dozen of those, from black leather to white Vegas silks—as well as statues depicting Drell triumphing at every sport possible.

"Uh-oh," muttered Hilda. "He's holding court in Ego Hall. That's usually a bad sign." Hilda knew Drell's moods better than almost anyone else. She had been engaged to marry him at one time, but he had left her waiting at the altar. Needless to say their relationship was in the "undefined" stage.

A red carpet with wide white fluffy edges ran from the closet door down an impossibly long aisle up to a gargantuan Victorian jurist's bench. When they walked forward onto the carpet, the distance was covered magically in just a few steps. This created the effect of having the judge's bench race toward them, growing ever larger and more impressive until they stood at its foot, staring up at scowling, bewigged Drell. He was flanked by bored-looking Cassandra and by Skippy, the silent overlord's underling. Skippy smiled brightly at Sabrina and waggled his fingers hello.

"Would you mind not standing on my periwig?" Drell sneered in his most sarcastic tone.

To her surprise, Sabrina realized that the fluffy edge of the carpet was actually one of the two side curls on Drell's English judge wig. She hopped onto the carpet with a flush of embarrassment.

"Is the persecuting attorney present?" Drell bellowed.

"Present and prepared," answered a higher pitched version of Drell's voice. Whirling to her right, Sabrina saw that it came from an animated bronze statue of Drell that stood behind a mahogany desk. The Judge Drell and Prosecutor Drell said in unison, "I'm the judge *and* the prosecutor—it's a cost-cutting thing."

* * *

Juniper Kelleigh took deep breaths and tried to calm herself. When she was a little girl she had tried to imagine herself in all the wonderful places described by the books her father painstakingly read to her. That yearning had expressed itself in a love of books, both the printed word and the paper that carried it.

Now here, in this place far stranger than any fantasy, the thing that struck her about the Spellman house was the unbelievable amount of *printing* it contained. There were hundreds of books just sitting casually on shelves—thick ones with stiff covers and smaller ones that had covers barely sturdier than the interior paper—newspapers and strange glossy booklets with vividly colored pictures, all of them obviously *printed*. There was even paper with printing on it in the tall bin for kitchen refuse. These people had paper enough to throw away!

Imagining how much learning, how much thought, how much of other people's experiences the witches had access to made her head swim. This glimpse of the future was heaven on earth for one such as Juniper.

Judge Drell grinned maliciously down from the bench. "Let's get on with the convictions, shall we?"

Salem jumped up on the defense table. "I represent the defense, Your Authoritarianship, sir. I move for a postponement until the court rules on a charge of violation of Rule 488."

The announcement caught Drell a little off guard. "And what is the nature of your 488?" he demanded.

"That on a perfectly legal and rule-abiding trip to the town of West Bridge in 1728, certain locals did falsely, knowingly, and maliciously prosecute a certifiably wax-sealed witch on the charges of witchcraft," Salem answered—rather well, he thought.

Drell laughed, and the volume of it could have shattered a double-pane window at a hundred paces. "What a coincidence! That trial is the very reason why I'm charging you and blondie over here with a violation of Rule 735! You instigated a witch trial at a time in history where a witch trial was never recorded *and* after witch trials had all but disappeared! You annoyed some unknown flunky and turned him into a crazed witch-hunter! Now, because you and blondie went on your little sight-seeing jaunt, all of American history is about to change!"

"We'll deal with that after you hear the 488 case."

"Why should your 488 take precedence over my 735?"

"Because it comes first," answered Salem. "That's what numerical order is all about."

Drell opened his mouth to protest, then paused and sat back. He flicked a quick glance over to

Cassandra and Skippy, who just shrugged at him. "Okay, furball, I'll make you a deal. We'll hold the trials simultaneously. You'll present your case; then I'll present mine. We'll take turns—just like checkers."

Sabrina leaned over to whisper in Salem's ear, "Are you crazy? That doesn't sound too good."

"Trust me," Salem hissed back. "I know what I'm doing!" Under his breath he added, "I think." He faced Drell and said loudly, "Deal."

"Let's get started, then, shall we?" Drell purred. He leaned forward to smile cruelly at Salem and Sabrina. "You realize, of course, that if you prove your 488, you'll automatically be admitting your guilt in the 735."

☆

Chapter 15

☆

Harvard Kinklin stood silently staring at the picture hanging on the kitchen corkboard. He had marveled at the stove and cutlery in the Spellmans' modern kitchen, and he'd even spent a long time staring out the windows at all the houses in the neighborhood. But of all the marvels in this strange world, he kept coming back to this one small image tacked to a wall.

In his native time, messages were strictly hand-written letters sent by carriage and post rider, so he wouldn't have understood the concept of a picture postcard. Yet he understood the images on the card before him, images somehow painted with no visible brushstrokes.

The postcard was divided into four quarters, each with a view of a different bridge over water. But what bridges! Spans that delighted the eye by seeming to swoop in great arcs, leaping from shore to shore. Trestles like iron muscles, bearing the weight of tons of roadbed with four-square strength. Harvard's eye traced their forms and tried to imagine their construction. The very existence of bridges like these spoke to him of endless roads chasing infinite horizons.

"You may present your case," boomed Drell.

A vellum scroll appeared to one side of the judge's bench. A golden quill pen hovered above the parchment, ready to record the legal proceedings for posterity.

Salem sat back on his haunches and brushed his whiskers slowly and dramatically. He leveled a hard stare at Drell and cleared his throat. "Your Omnipotent Despotness," he began. The quill scratched, and those words appeared on the scroll. "I intend to prove that one Magistrate Blackpoole, with the instigation and aid of one Mistress Libbeth Chestler, did falsely accuse Sabrina Spellman of being a witch and did furthermore lock me in a cage designed to hold a bird and did—"

"They're guilty," bellowed Drell. "You win. My turn."

Salem, carried away with the momentum of his argument, nearly fell off the defense table. "What?" he squawked. "I win? Just like that? But I had this whole speech prepared—"

"What can I say?" Drell smirked. "Your evidence spoke for itself. Now it's my turn. Prosecutor Drell?"

The bronze Drell raised his arm and called out, "The prosecution calls as its first and only witness the clerk of Möbius Trips."

The clerk appeared in the witness box and nodded gravely to Judge Drell. Bronze Drell approached him with clanking metallic steps.

"State your name for the record, please."

The clerk pursed his lips. "I can't rightly say that I have one," he replied.

Bronze Drell didn't expect that answer. "I beg your pardon?"

Judge Drell spoke to the floating pen. "Let the record show that the clerk is called the clerk because that's what we call him." The pen scribbled obediently.

Bronze Drell took another tack. "Clerk, do you recognize the defendants, Sabrina Spellman and Salem Saberhagen?"

"Yep. See them right in front of me, just like you do."

"And did they not, through your agency, travel back in time to the town of West Bridge in 1728, there to cause a temporal disturbance resulting in a witch trial of which there was no prior record?"

"Yes. No. Yes."

"Objection!" yelled Salem. "Witness is saying yes *and* no!"

"But he said yes twice and no once," boomed

Judge Drell. "Mathematically, that equals a yes. Objection overruled."

"Thank you, My Honor. You may step down," Bronze Drell told the clerk. He turned to face the bench. "My Alternate Self, I rest my case."

Once again Salem was taken by surprise. "Wha . . . what?" he sputtered.

Hilda hooted at the cat. "Great going, Salem! You're a regular Flea Bailey."

"Do you have a defense," taunted Judge Drell, "or shall we go straight to the sentencing?"

"Of c-course I have a defense," stammered Salem. "I call Libbeth Chestler and Magister Blackpoole to the stand."

"Denied," gloated Drell. "Mortals aren't permitted in the Other Realm, cat. Do you give up yet?"

Libbeth Chestler was the richest, most important girl in West Bridge. She owned the best things, wore the finest clothes, and dreamed of town houses in Boston. Things were satisfying to her only if they were better than what someone else had. No one could outdo Libbeth Chestler.

This house made Libbeth feel shabby. Everything she saw, everything she touched, even things that were obviously well used—all were finer than anything she or anyone she knew of owned.

An ache settled in her chest. The Spellman house—a house of witches!—would be an insult and a torment forever. Never again would she think of anything she owned without knowing that the most insignificant items in this house were better.

She wept bitter tears.

"Drell, may we have a short recess to consult with counsel here?" Zelda said, her voice tight as she glared at Salem.

"Sure, go ahead," Judge Drell said cheerfully. "Take all the time you want. It's all you've got left. Oh"—and he leaned forward—"did I forget to tell you that I'm charging you and your sister as accessories to the crime? You two are responsible for your little niece, remember." His laughter was a thing to chill ice cubes.

As the blood drained from her face, Zelda turned back to the others. Hilda was towering over Salem threateningly. "This is cutting it too close, buster," she snapped. "You'd better have a real ace up your sleeve to pull this off."

Salem blinked his round eyes and gulped. "Uh . . . sorry. No sleeves. I haven't a clue what to do next."

"You *what?* Ohh, if you weren't going to be disintegrated with the rest of us, I'd strangle you on the spot," Zelda growled.

"Come on, guys," pleaded Sabrina. "This is no time for fighting. Isn't there something we can do? I mean, look, if Salem and I had changed history, wouldn't we have noticed it? If yesterday wasn't the same as it *was* yesterday, we'd know it . . . or would we?"

"How can you say that stuff without tying your tongue in knots?" Salem complained. "You talk about time like that idiot clerk."

Sabrina's jaw dropped. "That's it! That's the answer!" she shouted. "Salem, don't ever change!"

"How can I?" the perplexed cat asked. "I'd have to know what I've done first."

Magister Blackpoole was lost in a nightmare worse than anything he could ever have imagined. The world was an unpredictable and dangerous place, one where crops failed, disasters befell the innocent, and epidemics wiped out whole communities. All his life his defense against all this rampaging chaos had been to try to impose order on everything around him. Fires kept carefully in hearths did not burn down houses. People kept under close control stayed organized and did not vanish in the wilderness. Society was safe only when people kept their natural places. His place, for example, was to be respected, feared, and obeyed without question.

But no one here was listening to him. They all ignored him as if his words were so many dandelion seeds in the wind, and in a house of vile witches where he should be his fellow townsfolk's main defense, their natural leader!

It was most disturbing, this den of witches. For one thing, it was remarkably tidy and tastefully decorated for a lair of agents of disorder. It was offensively eccentric, of course. Blackpoole hated novelty; he much preferred well-worn familiarity.

The other disturbing thing was the animated painting hearth. The witch called it "TV." Images and messages flickered in its strange black chest, images that appeared to be actual people, even though his hands told him that the surface was warm and unnaturally smooth glass. And then there were those words that appeared to be printed on the back of the glass, except that they changed as often as the images did. The language seemed to be English, but of a type so confounded that he was sure the intent was some form of dangerous evil.

And there was more, so much more to fear. Every person the hearth showed was different. Blackpoole had never seen people of so many varied shades and features. His skin crawled to see how men and women mingled shamelessly, how disorganized they looked, how aggressively . . . *individual* they all were. In his experience, no two people could see eye-to-eye on anything. Despite what the images tried to communicate, the streets of this strange future had to be filled with wars of disagreement. Chaos had always ruled the world, always would rule the world, and he was alone, utterly alone.

"Judge Drell . . ."

"Ah, Sabrina I'm-Too-Perky-for-My-Own-Good Spellman," oozed Drell. "Our cute little blond co-

conspirator. Did the cat flake out on you? He never was too good at planning ahead, you know."

"He did what he could," Sabrina declared, "considering you've rigged the trial as much as possible."

Drell casually waved his hands in the air. "Hey, it's one of the perks of being a despot. Are you going to take a swing at the plate, little girl?"

Sabrina clamped her jaw tight, then relaxed. "Just watch your outfield," she said defiantly. "I call as my first batter . . . I mean witness—"

"Not another mortal, is it?" Drell sneered, waggling a no-no finger at her.

Sabrina ignored the judge's interruption. "I call the clerk!"

"She's out of order. The clerk is *our* witness," objected Bronze Drell.

"Ah, but since he's already given testimony, you can't disqualify him without discrediting your own case," Sabrina pointed out. "Without his testimony, you haven't got a thing on us."

"Oh, let him take the stand," grumbled Judge Drell, "for all the good it'll do them. They're still guilty, and I'm going to disintegrate them one way or another."

The clerk reappeared in the witness box. "I've been getting pretty restive waiting for you to get around to this," he told Sabrina. Then he winked broadly at her.

"Objection!" shouted Bronze Drell. "Witness is winking at the accused!"

"Sorry," said the clerk. "Must be a mote in my eye."

"Now," said Sabrina, addressing the clerk. "You testified earlier about our trip back to 1728, is that correct?"

"Yep."

Bronze Drell clanged to attention. "Witness confirms the prosecution's case, Your Honor. I move we convict immediately!"

"I'm not done yet," Sabrina declared.

"Go on, go on," urged Judge Drell, looking bored. "Get it over with so I can disintegrate you soon. I have a big date tonight." He ignored the daggers shooting from Hilda's eyes at this.

Sabrina continued. "Tell us, Mr. Clerk, in your professional and expert opinion, did Salem or I change history in any way?"

The clerk grinned from ear to ear. "Nope. Not at all."

"What!" shrilled both Drells in unison.

"But you answered yes when I asked you if they'd disrupted history."

"I said yes, no, yes." The clerk smiled. "Yes, I sent them back in time. No, they didn't disrupt history. Yes, they did cause a trial . . . *that there was no record of having been held!"*

Pausing to enjoy the Drells' flabbergasted expressions, the clerk began what was obviously a speech he'd had long prepared. "History reveals that Hilda Spellman made her forget-me-knot a tad too strong. It not only made the townsfolk forget the previous two days, but it made everyone from the surrounding area forget about the town! For years nobody even remembered that West Bridge existed. People who lived there got used to it, didn't even notice it after a while. Just knew that the past wasn't a burden to them anymore. Even when the spell weakened, travelers passing through tended to forget they'd ever been there." He looked at Sabrina. "That's also why the Woodcutter building has always been a tavern or a restaurant or a pizza place. The remnants of the forget-me-knot have made that place a permanent refuge, a place where people can forget their cares."

"Then, in your expert opinion," Sabrina asked, hoping the answer would be what she wished, "are Salem and I guilty of time-tampering?"

The clerk beamed. "Nope," he proclaimed loudly. "And anyone who disagrees with me is absolutely inaccurate."

With a satisfied sigh, Sabrina said, "I rest my case, Drell."

Bronze Drell gnashed his metal teeth in fury. On the bench, Judge Drell fidgeted as both Skippy and Cassandra gave him the thumbs-up sign. If he held out, he was going to be outvoted by his own council. He grimaced and squeezed out, "Acquitted," almost inaudibly.

Zelda and Hilda rushed to hug Sabrina, the threat of disintegration dismissed. Salem harrumphed to get Drell's attention. "Your Absoluteness," he purred, "we still have the small matter of the punishment of the guilty in *my* case."

Drell clenched his fist and thunder rumbled overhead. "There! I disintegrated them."

To his vast surprise, a magical backlash threw him backward in his carved chair.

"Sorry," said the clerk. "Can't let you do that. Juniper Kelleigh has to become a very important pamphleteer during the American Revolution. Because people continually forgot about West Bridge, it made a perfect hiding place for her to print materials for the patriots right through the Revolution. And Harvard Kinklin has to go on and build a few dozen bridges in his life, starting with the one that will take him out of West Bridge forever."

"Hey, don't Blackpoole and Libbeth get punished for what they did to me?" whined Salem. "And to Sabrina, too, of course," he added belatedly.

"I've got special sealing wax that will seal their minds," said the clerk. "They won't be able to tell anyone a word about what they've seen in the future, but they won't forget it, either. That will be punishment enough for those two."

Thunder rumbled overhead again.

"Will you cut it out, Drell?" Hilda demanded angrily. "Just grow up!"

"It was an uninhabited galaxy! I had to disintegrate *something!*" snarled Drell. "Don't push me, Hilda!"

"Aren't you late for your big date?" she said cattily.

Drell's big body seemed to grow even bigger, inflating with fury. "Court is adjourned!" he roared in a thunderous voice. The Other Realm trembled, and the Spellmans and their cat were blasted back home.

☆

Chapter 16

Sabrina folded over the last page of her report c
colonial Westbridge and blinked at the applaus
from everyone in class except Libby Chessler.
was the first time she had completely forgotten th
she was reading a paper out loud. She set the pap
down neatly on Mrs. Hecht's desk and walked bac
the short distance to her front-row seat.

She reveled in the furious glare flaming fro
Libby's eyes. Even with a ghost-written paper, th
cheerleader's report couldn't hold a candle t
Sabrina's. The blond girl patted the leather-boun
book that sat on her desk as she thought of Junip
Kelleigh and Harvard Kinklin.

They'd had only a few minutes together befo
the colonists were whisked away back to their ow
time, but Sabrina had seen a peculiar spark in bo
pairs of eyes. Where Libbeth Chestler and Magist

Blackpoole had been sullen and moody on the Spellmans' return from the Other Realm, Juniper and Harvard had appeared somehow energized, even eager, and not at all afraid.

Sabrina had discovered Juniper's journal tucked away in her apron and had tried to return it. Juniper had refused it, saying, "I have the original. When I perfect my craft, I shall print more copies. Keep it as a reminder of where we all come from—brave, sometimes foolish people who desired to be more than they were."

Harvard had been too shy to say good-bye. Instead, he had blushed and muttered, "Knock-knock."

"Who's there?" Sabrina had replied.

"Interrupting cow."

"Interrupting cow wh—"

"Moo!" he blurted, turning away so she wouldn't notice his brimming eyes.

All too soon the clerk had appeared with his magic candles to seal their minds and transport them back to their native time. And all too soon as well it was Monday morning and time to deliver the report Sabrina had written about Juniper's book.

Mrs. Hecht was so delighted when Sabrina showed her the book that she didn't even question how it just happened to have been lying in her aunts' attic all these years.

And for Sabrina, history class would never be the same again. Now she could see the faces behind the gray type in her book. She could also see Libby's reflection in her compact mirror as she tousled Harvey's hair on her way forward to give her report. Sabrina gritted her teeth and kept her fingers from pointing.

There was plenty of time to get even.

About the Authors

DAVID CODY WEISS and BOBBI JG WEISS met and got married by mail, kind of like Sea Monkeys. At first they agreed never to send photographs to each other, so Bobbi thought David looked like Mel Gibson and David thought Bobbi looked like Flipper. It was a romance made in heaven, if you like fish.

When they finally met face-to-face, Bobbi was amazed to see that David looked about as much like Mel Gibson as a lightly buttered slice of sourdough toast did. Likewise, David was amazed to see that Bobbi really did look like Flipper. They could have opened a slam-dancing piano lounge, but they decided to become writing partners instead.

Among the books they've written are two other Sabrina, the Teenage Witch books; three Star Trek: Starfleet Academy novels *(Deceptions, Lifeline* and *Breakaway);* a Secret World of Alex Mack novel entitled *Close Encounters!;* and three Are You Afraid of the Dark? novels entitled *The Tale of the Shimmering Shell, The Tale of the Ghost Cruise* and *The Tale of the Stalking Shadow.* All are available from Archway Paperbacks and Minstrel Books.

David and Bobbi still hope to open that slam-dancing piano lounge one day, although they'll stick to writing for now (even though Bobbi has trouble typing with her fins).

@ café

Meet the staff of @café:
Natalie, Dylan, Blue, Sam, Tanya, and Jason.
They serve coffee, surf the net,
and share their deepest darkest secrets . . .

#1 Love Bytes
00445-X/$3.99

#2 I'll Have What He's Having
00446-8/$3.99

#3 Make Mine To Go
00447-6/$3.99

#4 Flavor of the Day
00448-4/$3.99

Novels by Elizabeth Craft

Available from Archway Paperbacks
Published by Pocket Books

POCKET
BOOKS

1430-02